"COME ON OUT. I'LL MAKE IT QUICK AND CLEAN," THE KILLER PROMISED WITH HUNGRY ANTICIPATION.

"I want to get this over with. *Come on!*"

The killer was moving slowly toward the jumble of granite. Zac didn't stand a chance. His hiding place was exposed in the full glare of the flashlight. The most he could hope to do was make a break for it, and Guinevere knew he'd never make it. He'd be cut down in a split second.

Fury overwhelmed her. She was on her feet before she had time to think, heaving her shoulder bag uselessly in the killer's direction. It fell short, but with jolting swiftness the flashlight was full on her, blinding her.

A shot slammed through the berry bushes and the flashlight swung wildly. She flattened herself against the muddy ground, waiting for the next shot. . . .

Other Guinevere Jones novels from Dell:

THE DESPERATE GAME
THE CHILLING DECEPTION
THE SINISTER TOUCH

Be sure to watch for other Dell Romantic Mystery/
Suspense Novels coming soon!

THE FATAL FORTUNE

Jayne Castle

A DELL BOOK

Published by
Dell Publishing Co., Inc.
1 Dag Hammarskjold Plaza
New York, New York 10017

Dell ® TM 681510, Dell Publishing Co., Inc.

ISBN: 0-440-12490-5

Printed in the United States of America

December 1986

10 9 8 7 6 5 4 3 2 1

DD

Chapter One

Guinevere Jones handed the sniffling young woman another tissue and waited for the newest spate of tears to halt. As she waited, she pushed the cup of tea closer to her companion's elbow, silently urging her to take another sip.

Tea and sympathy. It wasn't much to offer, under the circumstances, but until Sally Evenson had composed herself, there wasn't much else Guinevere could do. The two women were seated at the corner table in a small restaurant just off First Avenue in downtown Seattle. It was the middle of August and the temperature outside was in the mid seventies. The weather was perfect for dining at one of the outside tables, but that would be much too public for poor Sally in her present mood.

Sally Evenson had worked for Camelot Services as a temporary secretary for several months. Guinevere had sent her out on a number of jobs, and the frail-looking Sally had gained confidence and skill with each new assignment. She had been turning into one of Guinevere's most reliable temps, until disaster struck on the latest assignment. Guinevere still wasn't certain just what shape disaster had taken, because all Sally had been able to do for the past half hour was cry. Perhaps it was time to take a firm hand.

"All right, Sally, finish your tea and tell me exactly what's going on at Gage and Watson."

Sally raised her head, her eyes swollen and red. She was a young woman, twenty-three to be exact, painfully thin, and rather nervous in even the most serene situations. Some of that nervousness had been fading lately as Sally's job performance had improved. There had been a direct correlation between confidence and composure. Guinevere had been pleased at the transformation, but now it seemed all the progress had been undone.

"I can't talk about it, Miss Jones. You wouldn't understand. No one would understand. I'm sorry to bother you like this. I don't know what got into me. It's just that lately everything seems so . . . so impossible." Sally ducked her head again and blew her nose. Whatever claim to attractiveness the young woman had was submerged beneath the mournful wariness in her pale blue-green eyes and tautly drawn features. Her hair was an indeterminate shade of brown, worn in a short bob that badly needed a professional stylist's touch. She still wore her Camelot Services blazer, a smartly cut jacket of royal blue with the new Camelot Services crest on the left pocket.

Sally had fallen in love with the blazer the day Guinevere had given it to her. It was probably the most expensive garment she had ever had. Two months ago, Guinevere had hit on the idea of giving all her skilled, long-term employees jackets as a symbol of their elite status in the temporary service field. The blazers were slowly but surely becoming an emblem of the best in temporary help in the Seattle business community. Camelot Services employees wore them with pride. It was good advertising, Guinevere told herself each time she wrote out a corporate check for another of the expensive blazers.

Guinevere took a sip of coffee and set the cup down gently but firmly. "Sally, I can't help you if you don't tell me what's going on. Now, it's been obvious for the past couple of weeks that you've developed personal problems. I do not believe in getting involved in my employees' problems—unless they affect job performance. Unfortunately, your problem has gotten to that stage. If you don't pull yourself together, I'm going to have to take you off the Gage and Watson job. You know it and I know it."

Sally stared at her with horror. "Oh, please, Miss Jones, don't do that. I love the job, and my manager at Gage and Watson says it could go on for a couple more months. I need the money. I've moved into a new apartment, and I was going to go shopping for some clothes and I wanted to buy a new stereo—"

"All right, all right," Guinevere said gently, holding up a hand to stem the flow of protest. "I realize you need the job. And I need you on it. You've been doing excellent work. Gage and Watson assures me they're very pleased. I wouldn't be surprised if when this assignment is over they offer you full-time employment."

Sally's face lit up. "Do you really think so? Oh, Miss Jones, that would be fabulous. A real, full-time job. A *career*." For a moment she was lost in blissful contemplation of a future in which she had a career.

Guinevere smiled wryly. "Gage and Watson's gain will be my loss."

Sally's excitement dissolved on the spot. Guiltily she dabbed at her eyes. "Of course. I forgot. If I were to get a full-time job at Gage and Watson I'd no longer be able to work for you on a temporary basis, would I? I'm sorry, Miss Jones, I didn't stop to think. I owe everything to you. I wouldn't dream of leaving you, after all you've done for me."

Guinevere grinned. "You most certainly will leave me, when the right full-time position comes along. It's called 'career advancement,' Sally, and, although I'll hate to lose you, I have absolutely no intention of holding you back. Don't worry. Happens all the time in the temporary help field. I'm used to it." Which didn't mean she liked it, but she was businesswoman enough to accept the inevitable. Besides, sending out temps who were good enough to hire on permanently at the offices where they had been assigned was just another example of sound advertising. As she was always telling Zac, you had to look on the positive side.

Sally smiled tremulously. "You're so understanding, Miss Jones."

"I'm trying to be, Sally. I'm trying. Now, tell me what's gone wrong at Gage and Watson."

The young woman hesitated, and then confided in a rush, "It's got nothing to do with Gage and Watson. Gage and Watson is a wonderful company, Miss Jones."

"Is it the people you're working with? Is some man hassling you on the job? There are laws against that, you know," Guinevere said bluntly.

"Oh, no, nothing like that." Sally gave her a pathetic glance. "I'm not exactly the sort of woman men would hassle on the job, you know."

"No, I do not know. You're an attractive, single woman. Unfortunately, job harrassment occurs even at the best firms. But if it's not the people at Gage and Watson who are causing you trouble, what is it? If it's something too personal to talk about to me, then maybe you should consider some counseling, Sally, because whatever it is, it's starting to ruin everything you've been working so hard on for the past few months."

Sally bit her lip. "I . . . I am getting counseling, Miss Jones."

Guinevere's eyebrows went up. "You are?"

"Well, of a sort. I mean, Madame Zoltana is a kind of counselor. She's very intelligent, and she . . . she sees things, you know? But she's kind of expensive, and lately I've been having to see her a lot." Sally reached for a few more tissues to blot the new flow of tears.

"Madame Zoltana?" Guinevere stared at Sally. "That doesn't sound like a counselor's name or title. Who on earth is Madame Zoltana?"

"She's a psychic," Sally explained uneasily, not looking at Guinevere. "Several people at Gage and Watson go to her. Francine Bates introduced me to her a few weeks ago. She has a great gift—Madame Zoltana, that is, not Francine. It's absolutely incredible what she can see. She can tell you so many things about your past that sometimes it's frightening."

Sally looked frightened, all right, Guinevere decided abruptly. Frightened, and alone in the world. A very scared young woman. "Tell me, Sally, exactly what Madame Zoltana does when you go to see her."

Sally's lower lip trembled. She stared down into her teacup. "She sees things. She warns you about things that might happen if you aren't careful. Then she . . . she helps you."

"Helps you?"

The young woman nodded bleakly. "She can sometimes change things for you. Things that . . . that might go wrong."

Guinevere swore silently to herself. "And she'll help you avoid these things that might go wrong, as long as you continue seeing her on a regular basis, I suppose?"

Sally nodded, looking up with a kind of sad fear in her tear-filled eyes. "I do try to see her regularly, Miss Jones. But as I said, she's very expensive, and last week when I explained to her that I might not be able to pay her fees, she said that unless I did, the most awful thing would happen."

"What did she say would happen, Sally?"

Sally Evenson collapsed into fresh tears. When she finally stopped crying, she told Guinevere exactly what threat hung over her frail, young head.

Guinevere was still fuming when she got back to the office an hour later. Trina Hood, the temp Guinevere used to help out in Camelot Services' own offices, looked up with a cheerful smile.

"Mr. Justis called. He said to remind you that you promised to help him deal with the caterer tonight after work. I think he's getting nervous, Miss Jones."

"Zac hasn't ever given an office reception," Guinevere explained mildly as she sat down at her desk and sifted through a small stack of messages. "He's going through the usual party-giver's panic, wondering if he'll wind up spending a fortune on food and champagne and have no one show up. Did he say what time he wanted to meet me?"

Trina nodded. "He said he'll come by to collect you around five."

"Collect me?"

"I think that was the word he used. He instructed me not to let you get away."

Guinevere smiled fondly. "Poor Zac. Amazing how a man with all his talents is reduced to fear and trembling by the mere thought of giving a party. Anything else crucial happen while I was gone?"

"Two more calls for clerks needed for vacation fill-ins. I've already contacted two people in our files. Both said they'd report to work at the firms tomorrow morning."

"Great." Guinevere smiled approvingly at Trina. She had used a handful of different people from her own staff during the past few weeks, in an attempt to find someone who would work out on a full-time basis. After her sister Carla had left to set up her own art gallery in Pioneer Square, Guinevere had discovered just how much she had come to rely on full-time office help at Camelot Services.

Trina Hood was showing definite potential. She was a pleasant woman in her mid forties who had recently been divorced and now had two children to raise alone. There was a certain comfortable plumpness about her, and she had an excellent telephone voice. She was also a hard worker and anxious to please. As she had explained to Guinevere, she had been out of the work force for almost ten years, and she had been terrified of the prospect of having to find a job. She had decided to start out as a Camelot temp, to get her feet wet in the business world. She had walked through the doors of Camelot Services on the very day Guinevere had acknowledged to herself that she wasn't going to be able to get by with part-time help. Guinevere had grabbed her.

"What about Gage and Watson, Gwen? Want me to find someone to replace Sally Evenson?" Trina asked quietly. She was well aware that things were shaky.

Guinevere thought for a moment. "No," she said finally, "I think I'll go over to Gage and Watson myself for a few days. Something is bothering Sally, and I want to check out the situation there. Can you find her another short-term assignment? She needs to work."

Trina nodded. "Gallinger Industries needs a typist for a few days."

"Put Sally on it."

"I don't get it. You're going to go into Gage and Watson yourself?"

"That's right. I'll tell Gage and Watson that Sally is ill, and that I'm her replacement."

"Well, all right, but I don't understand why you want to take one of your own temporary assignments. What about running things here?"

"For that I'll rely on you, Trina."

Zac showed up in the doorway of Camelot Services at five minutes after five. It was obvious he had walked straight down the hill from his own small office in a Fourth Avenue high rise. He had his conservatively tailored jacket hooked over one shoulder. His crisp, white shirt fit him well, emphasizing the solid, compact strength of his shoulders and the flat planes of his stomach.

Zachariah Justis, president and sole employee of Free Enterprise Security, Inc., would never win any male beauty contests. The first time Guinevere met him, she had labeled him a frog. It wasn't that he was as ugly as a frog, it was just that he had been surrounded at the time by a bar full of young, beautiful, upwardly mobile types, and in their midst he had stood out quite prominently. Add to that the fact that shortly after he'd introduced himself to Guinevere, he'd coerced her into helping him in an investigation, and one could understand why she had been less than enthusiastic about Zac Justis.

Zac was just under six feet tall, a compactly built man with short, almost military-style night-dark hair and cool, ghost-gray eyes. He was thirty-six years old, but it had struck Guinevere on occasion that those years must have been years of hard-fought experience. Sometimes she wanted to ask him more about his past, but he usually showed no interest in discussing it, so she tended to back off the subject. Among the few facts she did know was that Zac had spent several years working for a large, multinational security firm before starting his own small business in Seattle.

She could guess at some aspects of his past, because she had witnessed some of his more unique skills. She had, for example, seen him make the transition from businessman to cold, lethal hunter on more than one occasion, and it gave her chills to think of the kind of life he must have led before settling down in Seattle. Guinevere still wasn't certain why she had fallen in love with the man. She only knew that her life was never going to be the same now that Zachariah Justis was in it.

They had begun their relationship as adversaries, but the tension between them had quickly exploded into passion. Passion had led to an affair, and then to love. It was a very new, cautiously admitted love, something that they had both finally acknowledged only a couple months previously. They didn't talk about it very much. There was still a sense of wonder and uncertainty about the relationship, as far as she was concerned. In true male fashion, however, Zac seemed to take everything for granted now. That was typical of Zac. He had a blunt, straightforward approach to most things—including, apparently, falling in love.

Guinevere reminded herself on occasion that there was much she didn't know about Zachariah Justis. The reverse was true, too, but Guinevere doubted that a complete résumé of her past would contain any earthshaking surprises for Zac. However, she wondered what she would learn if she were to see a detailed résumé of *his* past. She told herself philosophically that the early stages of love were a time of discovery. It was not a time to be rushed. She would continue feeling her way, learning what she could about Zachariah Justis.

"The caterer said he'd see us at five thirty," Zac announced as he came through the door. "Let's get going."

"Relax, Zac. He's only a couple of blocks away. We'll get there in plenty of time." Guinevere picked up her shoulder bag and glanced around the office. "Besides, I want to talk to you. I need some professional advice."

Zac waited impatiently by the door, his eyes turning suddenly suspicious. "Professional advice? What sort of advice? Gwen, I don't want you getting mixed up in any more crazy investigations. I can find my own clients. I don't need you to dig up more work for me."

She smiled in what she hoped was a reassuring way. "Calm down. I'm not asking you to take on any investigations. This one I'm going to handle on my own. I just want some advice from you, that's all." She playfully pushed him out into the hall and locked the office door.

"Gwen, I mean it, I've got enough to do during the next couple of weeks without having to chase after you trying to keep you out of trouble. I've got this damn reception to plan, and the move to my new office to supervise. On top of everything else, I'm supposed to be interviewing for a secretary. That reminds me— why haven't you sent anyone over for me to talk to?"

"I'm still selecting the final candidates. A good secretary is hard to find, Zac. It takes time. Trust me."

"Uh-huh. Are you sure you're not being a little too picky?" He took her arm and steered her forcefully down the stairs and out onto the sidewalk.

"Zac, I have to be picky. You're not going to be the easiest man to work for, you know. You need someone calm and unflappable. Someone with a good personality, so that she can handle your important clients properly. You also need someone who can do your typing, handle your accounts, and present a good image."

"Damn it, Gwen, I just want a secretary, not a presidential aide."

"Don't worry, Zac, I'll send someone over soon. Now, about my little problem—"

"Guinevere, I have learned through hard experience that your problems are rarely *little.*"

"Don't sound so abused. I'm not going to involve you in this. I've told you, I just want some advice. Now, here's the situation: I think one of my employees has become the victim of a very subtle, very cruel protection racket."

Zac slid her a sidelong glance. "Are you kidding?"

"No. Listen to this and tell me what you think. I sent a young woman over to Gage and Watson a few weeks ago."

"The electronics firm?"

Guinevere nodded. "Someone in her office turned her on to a psychic, a character who goes by the name of Madame Zoltana. Madame Zoltana agreed to see her initially for a small consulting fee, but after a couple of visits she revealed to poor little Sally that she knew Sally had gotten pregnant when she was seventeen."

"Oh, hell." Zac sounded as if he knew what was coming.

"Sally was flabbergasted. It seemed to prove that Madame Zoltana really knew her stuff. But it didn't stop there. Zoltana also knew that Sally had given the baby up for adoption. You have to understand, Zac, that the experience nearly devastated Sally. She's a fragile person, in the first place. Finding herself pregnant and abandoned at seventeen nearly caused her to commit suicide. She was talked into having the baby by one of those antiabortion groups. They promised her that once she gave the baby away she would be free to rebuild her own life. Sally did exactly that. It's been a long, slow process. Because of the baby, she was forced to drop out of school. She had to complete high school through a GED program. Her parents disowned her, and she was left destitute. It's a sad story. Suffice it to say that she's gradually pulled herself back together. A few months ago she came to work for me, and she's shown remarkable improvement on the job. She's starting to come into her own at last."

"Guinevere, the social worker," Zac commented dryly.

"I'm serious, Zac. That young woman really started to get her act together during the past few months. For the first time since she was seventeen, she's beginning to see a future for herself. But she's still very fragile, Zac. Now along comes this screwy Madame Zoltana and warns her that her whole world is about to fall apart again."

"How?"

Guinevere drew a deep breath. "She told Sally that unless Sally kept coming to her on a regular basis, the baby she gave away when she was seventeen would someday learn who its natural mother is, come looking for her, and ruin Sally's life. For the right price, Madame Zoltana says, she can prevent that from happening with her psychic powers. Poor little Sally is absolutely terrified."

Zac whistled softly. "I'll be damned. That's pretty grim, all right. What a racket."

"That's exactly what it sounds like to me, a sleazy sort of protection racket. Madame Zoltana finds some

17

useful secret in a person's past and then offers 'protection'—for a price."

"And the price is continued visits to Madame Zoltana at very high fees."

"Exactly." Guinevere lifted her chin determinedly. "I can't allow that sort of thing to happen to one of my employees on the job, Zac. I'm going to find out what's going on and expose the whole sordid mess. That Madame Zoltana deserves to be hung."

Zac sighed. "Gwen, if people are stupid enough to believe in psychics and dumb enough to pay them, there's just not much you can do about it. About all you can do is explain to Sally what's going on, and hope she'll be smart enough to believe you."

"Poor Sally is too distraught to know what to believe. I've got to prove Zoltana is a fraud."

"Be reasonable, Gwen. How are you going to do that?"

"The way I figure it," Guinevere said thoughtfully, "Zoltana must have some inside help at Gage and Watson. Sally's not the only G and W employee who's seeing her, and from what I can gather, a couple of the others have been getting the same treatment. Somehow, Zoltana spots the gullible ones and then finds out something she can use against them."

Zac lifted one eyebrow. "Inside help?"

"Yeah. You know, someone who works at Gage and Watson, someone who potential victims might confide in. Whoever it is then passes the information along to Zoltana. From what Sally told me today, that would seem to be the way things work."

"Gwen, do you mind if I pont out that you've got a company to run? You can't make a career out of ex-

18

posing fraudulent psychics, believe me. Houdini tried, and it didn't do much good. There are always going to be some people who *want* to believe in charlatans like Zoltana. As long as there are believers, there will be frauds."

"All I want is a little advice from you, Zac. I thought you could give me some pointers on how to go about exposing a fraud."

"As usual," Zac said with a long-suffering sigh, "my advice to you is to *stay out of it.* But, as usual, I suppose you won't pay any attention."

Guinevere smiled contentedly. "I knew you'd help me."

"Wait a minute. I never said I'd help."

"Now, Zac, I'm approaching you in a professional capacity here."

"The hell you are. You're just trying to get some free assistance," he shot back.

"Well, you owe me something for all the help I'm giving you planning your reception," Guinevere informed him as they reached the entrance of a trendy delicatessen-restaurant on Western Avenue. "Here we are. We can discuss my case later. Now, remember what I told you about dealing with this caterer, Zac. I don't want you making a fuss every time I mention French champagne or good pâté. If you're going to have a proper reception for your clients, you have to do it right. You must go first class."

"Easy for you to say. It's not your money."

"Quit complaining. This is going to be a wonderful party. Great PR for Free Enterprise Security."

"What if no one shows up?" he demanded, holding open the door for her.

"Then you and I will have a lot of food and champagne to take care of. Might take us the rest of the year!"

"Gwen!" Horrified, he hurried after her, catching up just as she hailed the young chef with whom they had an appointment.

"Hello, Charles," Guinevere said cordially. "I think we're ready to make the final decisions. Zac has made it clear he wants everything to be just right, so please feel free to advise us." She ignored Zac's groan of despair and led the two men toward a vacant table.

"I am sure you will be quite pleased, Mr. Justis," Charles assured him, taking out a pen and a long pad of paper. "Shall we deal with the canapés and pâtés first? We have an excellent lobster pâté I would like to suggest. It's a specialty of the restaurant, and we do it exceedingly well."

"Lobster?" Zac's voice sounded strained. *"Lobster?"*

"I think the lobster is a wonderful suggestion, Charles," Guinevere offered swiftly. "I also think we should feature some salmon, don't you?"

"Salmon is always popular," Charles agreed, scribbling rapidly. "And we do a truly superior salmon hors d'oeuvre, which features just a touch of dill and caper. I'm sure you'll like it."

Zac knew there was no room in this conversation for him. He sat back in his chair, watching dolefully as Guinevere blithely ran up the tab for the reception he was planning. Hard to believe that initially it was just an off-the-cuff suggestion he'd made, when he'd decided to move the offices of Free Enterprise Security into a suite higher up in his office building. Business had been improving for his firm lately, and Zac was anxious to move up in the world. Time to get a real office, a view, and a secretary. One had to think of the image. And wouldn't it be nice maybe to invite some of his clients to a little reception to celebrate?

Guinevere had assured him it was a brilliant notion. The next thing Zac knew he was planning a no-expense-spared party. The formal announcements had gone out last week. Guinevere had sent a clerk over to help him address the envelopes. After that, he was committed. Panic had set in almost at once. Now he was beyond panic. He had placed himself in Guinevere's hands, and lord only knew what the result would be. One thing was certain. He was going to be a lot poorer when it was all over.

But that was the thing about Guinevere Jones. Life hadn't been the same for Zac since he had met her. And when all was said and done, he knew he wouldn't ever want to go back to the way things had been before she had entered his world. Zac tended to take a realistic, pragmatic view of life and of himself. He knew himself well enough, for example, to know he'd do anything to keep Guinevere safe. It was a measure of the differences between them that she would undoubtedly be shocked if she knew that. As far as Zac was concerned, it was just a fact of life.

Chapter Two

The headquarters of Gage and Watson occupied two floors in a Second Avenue high rise that was only three blocks from Guinevere's own office. She checked in at Camelot Services to make certain Trina was on top of the early morning rush, and then she walked up the hill to Second Avenue.

It had been a while since Guinevere had gone out on one of her company's assignments. In the beginning she had done it frequently, rather than have to turn down a job from an important client. But Camelot Services was getting bigger, and her employees more diversified and efficient. It was rare these days that she found herself having to fill in on a moment's notice.

But this situation was different, Guinevere reminded herself as she walked through the revolving doors and into the two-story lobby of the building. This time she was undertaking her own investigation. This was her first, very own big case. She couldn't wait until she could put the results in front of Zac. He was going to have to admit that she had definite talent in the investigative business. Besides, she thought, as she rode the elevators up to the nineteenth floor, where she was to report in for work, this whole thing was going to be rather exciting. She would be on her own this time around. Damned if she would ask Zac Justis for any more advice. Zac could be a wet blanket at times—usually when she was really getting excited or involved in something of which he did not approve. Zac didn't seem to realize just how many things there were in this world of which he didn't approve.

On the nineteenth floor, Guinevere stepped out of the elevator into the lobby of Gage and Watson. There was the usual confusion at the reception desk while the receptionist sorted out the situation. After three phone calls the woman looked up with a cheerfully relieved smile.

"You're to report in to Miss Malcolm at the end of the hall. She's in charge of the typists and word processors."

"Thank you," Guinevere said politely, and turned in the direction indicated. She ducked into a ladies' room halfway down the hall and double-checked her appearance in the mirror. The royal blue blazer fit like a glove, nipping in slightly at her slender waist and causing her small bust to appear a bit fuller than nature had ordained. Guinevere had had her own blazer especially tailored and hadn't regretted the expense. With the blazer, she wore a narrow tan skirt that fit smoothly over her hips. She considered this portion of her anatomy a bit too well-rounded, although Zac certainly didn't seem to mind. Zac, however, tended toward an earthy view, and his taste couldn't be relied on when it came to matters of fashion and style.

Guinevere frowned slightly at her image, turning her head a little to make sure the neat coffee-brown hair was still firmly knotted at the nape of her neck. Smiling at the small Camelot Services crest on her pocket, she turned and walked out of the ladies' room —and promptly collided with the man in the corridor outside. So much for professional decorum.

"Excuse me," Guinevere mumbled hastily, disengaging herself and stooping quickly to pick up the file folder she had just dropped. "Very clumsy of me. They ought to put mirrors up across the hall, so that when you open the door, you know what's coming!"

"If I'd known who was coming out of the rest room," the man said as he bent down to help her with the folder, "I'd have made certain I was standing exactly where I was. As it is, I guess I was just lucky. Hello, Guinevere Jones. It's been a long time."

Guinevere's fingers tightened convulsively around the folder as shock went through her. She raised her head and slowly got to her feet. There were several skills one learned when one ran a service-oriented business. One of them was how to smile even though you were recovering from stunned amazement. She called upon that skill now. "Hello, Rick. What a surprise. I had no idea you worked for Gage and Watson."

"For almost a year now," Rick Overstreet answered easily. His golden-brown eyes moved over Guinevere with interested appraisal. "What are you doing here? A couple of years ago I had the impression you were planning to go into business for yourself."

Guinevere had forgotten just how intimate Rick's glances could be. He had the unsettling ability of making a woman feel pinned like a butterfly beneath his gaze. Overstreet was forty by now, she figured, and he had definitely aged well. His body was still austerely lean and obviously in good shape. He wore his expen-

24

sive business suit well. The thick, tawny-brown hair was laced with a hint of gray at the temples, giving him a sophisticated, male-in-his-prime look that complemented the straight nose, firm mouth, and strong jaw. His features were regular and well fashioned, strong and masculine, but it had always been his eyes that had attracted women. Rick Overstreet had the eyes of a big, tawny cat. He also had the morals of one, as far as Guinevere was concerned.

"My business is doing fine," she told him calmly. "But we're a little busy at the moment, so I'm taking one of the field assignments. If you'll excuse me, I should be moving along. Professional temps are never supposed to be late, you know. Nice to see you again, Rick."

He smiled lazily. "How about coffee later this morning?"

"Thanks, but I'm probably going to have to work straight through," she lied. "I understand the Gage and Watson typing pool is swamped this week. I'm here to help with the overload. How's your wife?" Guinevere asked with cool bluntness.

Rick's smile disappeared, and he fished out a pack of cigarettes, the expensive French brand he had favored two years ago. "Elena died almost two years ago. Shortly after you and I stopped seeing each other, in fact." He lit the cigarette with a small gold lighter.

The news of Elena's death jolted Guinevere. "I'm sorry, Rick. I didn't know."

"It's been two years. I don't think about it too much anymore. She died in a car accident on her way to Portland to see her family."

Guinevere nodded, not knowing what to say. She

had never met Elena Overstreet; hadn't known of the woman's existence until it was almost too late. "Well, good-bye, Rick. I really must be going." She turned away and moved hurriedly down the hall, aware of Rick Overstreet's golden eyes following her into a large room at the end of the corridor. The moment she was out of his sight she realized she was breathing too quickly, as if she had been running. Guinevere forced herself to take a deep, calming breath, as a business-like, auburn-haired woman in her thirties came forward with a smile.

"You must be Miss Jones, from the agency. Very glad to see you. I understand your typing is excellent. We were worried when we learned that Sally was ill, but Camelot Services assured us someone would be along to replace her. You wouldn't happen to know anything about word processors, too, would you?"

Guinevere smiled at the familiar question. "I'm reasonably familiar with the standard office models." She glanced around and saw what brand was in use at Gage and Watson. "I think I can manage."

"Thank goodness. We could have used you as a typist, but frankly, you'll be far more useful on the word processor. Come over here and meet Francine Bates. She'll show you the ropes."

Francine Bates was everyone's idea of a mother figure. Warm, slightly plump, her gray hair worn in a soft halo around her smiling features, she might have just stepped out of the kitchen with a tray of cookies and milk. Guinevere remembered vaguely that Sally Evenson had mentioned her.

"Sit down, and I'll show you what we're doing," Francine invited cheerfully. "Don't worry, Lisa," she added to the typing pool supervisor. "I'll have her up and running in no time. Do you want her to start on the Copperfield report?"

"That would be great," Lisa Malcolm said. "It's due on Friday." She smiled and went off to organize the early morning chaos at the other end of the room.

"I appreciate the help," Guinevere said, tucking her shoulder bag into her desk drawer as she sat down in front of the word processor.

"No problem. You're from the same agency little Sally Evenson was from, aren't you? I recognize the jacket."

"That's right. Sally had to take the rest of the week off. I'm filling in for her."

Francine nodded. "Sally's a sweet thing, a sensitive young woman. I've enjoyed working with her for the past few weeks. I hope she's all right?"

"Oh, yes. Just a slight cold."

Francine clucked sympathetically as she arranged papers on Guinevere's desk. "Such a frail little thing. Probably doesn't take much to make her ill. I told her she wasn't eating properly. Lord knows what she does eat. Probably just fast food. I've thought about taking her over to my sister's place on the coast for a few days. My sister's a great cook. She could put a little meat on Sally's bones. Well, back to business, here's what the big rush is all about," she went on, pointing to the papers she had placed on the desk. "This report is due on Friday. Of course, management didn't get it to us until the last minute, and there have been changes almost every day. I don't know how they expect us to do a final version by Friday, when they're

27

probably still going to be making revisions on Thursday night. But I guess that's management for you."

"Yes," Guinevere agreed feelingly, "that's management."

The work occupied Guinevere throughout the morning. During that time she met the other people who worked in the office, all of whom were women. She was invited to accompany Francine Bates and a few of the others on coffee break in the building cafeteria and accepted the invitation with alacrity. She wanted to become part of the group as quickly as possible, not only because it was company policy for a Camelot Services employee to be friendly, but because it would be the fastest way to make the contact with Madame Zoltana.

The conversation at coffee break covered everything from troublesome teenagers to the new fall styles showing up in the local department stores. Guinevere listened and participated while she sipped her coffee, but she was disappointed when no one mentioned Madame Zoltana. That was the thing about undercover investigations, she decided. You had to have patience. Hadn't Zac always told her that? Unfortunately, patience was not one of her virtues.

Guinevere glanced at her watch as she thought of Zac. She was due to meet him for lunch. She had vowed she wouldn't ask him for any more advice, but she decided to change her mind. Perhaps he could suggest some method of bringing up the subject of Madame Zoltana without arousing suspicion. She'd probably have to listen to another lecture on not getting involved, but it would be worth it if she got some useful pointers.

Zac left his office a few minutes before noon and strolled down to Second Avenue to pick up Guinevere for lunch. He was pleased with the way plans were going for his big move up. The movers had promised to arrive on the specified day and the new furniture was already in a warehouse, waiting to be delivered. As far as Zac could see, there were no real glitches on the horizon in the moving department, but he knew that some were bound to develop. It was a law of nature.

The real problem was getting Guinevere to send him some secretarial candidates. He was beginning to think he'd made a mistake, asking her to handle the initial interviews. At the time it had seemed reasonable enough. After all, she was the expert at hiring secretaries, and she had a whole stable of them to draw on. But so far he hadn't been presented with a single live choice, and it was beginning to worry Zac. What was the holdup? He wanted the secretary to move into the new office suite on the same day that the furniture was installed. Zac liked things neat and tidy.

The August sun was heating the city to a mellow seventy-eight degrees. As he neared the high rise where Guinevere was working, he removed his jacket and slung it over his shoulder. Perhaps it would be a good day to eat at one of the restaurants in the Pike Place Market. Zac considered the matter closely as he approached the revolving doors of the building. He was hungry. Through narrowed eyes he spotted a blue blazer among a crowd of people stepping out of an elevator, as he walked into the cool lobby.

Guinevere didn't notice him immediately. She was

talking to a man who had exited the elevator beside her. Zac watched the two of them cross the wide slate lobby floor, and something tightened inside him. Guinevere was smiling but there was something unnatural about her normally warm, charming smile. Zac frowned at the way the man's tawny head was bent toward her. He got the impression Guinevere's companion was trying to talk her into something. Probably lunch.

Impelled by a distinctly primitive need to stake his claim in front of the other man, Zac went forward purposefully. "Hi, Gwen. Ready for lunch?" His voice was a low-pitched, gravelly sound that was meant to catch the attention of both parties. It did.

Guinevere's reaction startled Zac. She turned her head at once, something akin to relief in her eyes. Then she was hurrying toward him, her high heels clicking on the slate floor. "Oh, there you are, Zac. I'm ready." The smile was as full of relief as her eyes, and she did something she almost never did in public. She came to a halt in front of him, stood on her toes, and kissed him.

Zac recovered almost instantly from the shock, and took her arm with possessive force. He was intensely aware of the tawny-haired man watching them. Zac glanced back casually as he guided Guinevere toward the door, and his gaze collided with that of the watching man. Zac decided he didn't like him at all. Coolly he turned his back on him and ushered Guinevere through the revolving doors.

"Who was that?" he asked without preamble as they reached the sidewalk.

"Nobody important. Just someone who works for

Gage and Watson," Guinevere said quickly. "Where are we going?"

"How about down to the market?" Was she brushing off his question because she had no interest in the man who had stepped out of the elevator with her, or because she didn't want to discuss him?

"That sounds fine. I feel like pasta today."

"You always feel like pasta," he reminded her indulgently.

So they ate pasta in a trendy little café, and afterward they wandered back through the vegetable stalls that lined the cobbled street of the Pike Place Market. Guinevere bought two plump peaches for dessert and sliced them with a plastic knife. It was tricky eating the juicy fruit on the sidewalk, but there was something pleasantly romantic about the business too, Zac decided. Lately he had been more and more aware of the feeling of being one half of a couple. It was the first time in his life he had felt like this. Guinevere Jones was occasionally infuriating, frequently charming, often recklessly impulsive, but above all, she was his. She belonged to him now, Zac reminded himself complacently. She was in love with him. And he was in love with her.

This business of being in love was still new to both of them, Zac realized. They were both learning the parameters of the commitment, discovering its depths, being careful not to rush through the fascinating discoveries they were making. Maybe this was the reward for waiting, and falling in love in your thirties, instead of at eighteen. You were more aware of the subtler aspects of the whole process. On the other hand, Zac decided, subtlety wasn't always such a great thing. It left small questions unanswered.

But there were certain straightforward questions that could still be asked. Zac finished his peach and wiped his hands on a paper napkin. "What time are you serving dinner tonight?"

Guinevere made a face. "Oh, Zac, you're so romantic."

He grinned. "You're going to owe me a lot of dinners for the next few weeks. I intend to get something in exchange for all the Free Enterprise Security cash you're spending on the party."

Trina Hood was still in the office when Guinevere returned to Camelot Services after work that day. She looked up with a glimmer of mischief in her eyes as her boss came through the door. "I think I've found her, Gwen."

"Found who?" Guinevere went to her desk to sort through the messages.

"The new secretary for your friend Zac."

Guinevere's head came up quickly. "You did?"

"Uh-huh. And she's perfect, Gwen. You aren't going to be able to find fault with her, the way you have with all the others. If Zac knew how many secretarial candidates you've turned down on his behalf, he'd explode."

Guinevere frowned thoughtfully, sitting down. "Now, Trina, you know I'm only trying to be careful. Zac will probably be a difficult employer. He can be short-tempered, dictatorial, and difficult. No one knows that better than I. It will take a very calm, mature person to work in his office."

Trina was trying to stifle a broad grin. "By calm, you mean placid, and by mature, you mean someone over fifty, right? You can't kid me, Guinevere Jones. You've turned down every potential candidate for a week, because each one has been cute and under thirty."

"Zac doesn't need an ex-cheerleader in his office," Guinevere informed her loftily.

"He needs someone who can type and answer phones. Ninety percent of the people you've interviewed could probably have handled the job, Gwen." Trina held up a hand. "But don't worry, I understand, even if Zac wouldn't. This time you don't have to fret. Evelyn Pemberton is exactly what you want for Zac. She's fifty-three, well groomed, intelligent, well mannered, and poised. She's also happily married, with grandchildren."

"How's her typing?"

Trina pretended to look surprised. "I didn't know that was as important as the fact that she's not likely to seduce Zac."

Guinevere laughed ruefully. "Have I been so obvious?"

"Just a tad, but I won't tell. Evelyn Pemberton types seventy-five words a minute. Flawlessly. I tested her on your machine."

"Okay, Trina. Set up an appointment with her for me." Guinevere leaned forward to study her calendar. "How about on my lunch hour tomorrow?"

"I already have," Trina informed her blandly. "I made one for her with Zac for the day after tomorrow."

"You're that sure?"

"I'm positive this is the one you've been looking for, Gwen. Take my word for it. But you know, you've been worrying needlessly about putting temptation in Zac's office. I've seen the way that man looks at you. He's got a one-track mind, and that applies to his love life, as well as everything else. You're the only woman on the track."

Guinevere sighed. "I just want to make sure it stays that way."

That night after dinner Guinevere told Zac she thought his opening for a secretary was about to be filled. It gave her a marvelously self-righteous feeling to be able to say that Trina Hood had found the likely candidate. This way Zac couldn't accuse her of being too picky. Curled up beside him on the black leather couch in her brightly colored apartment, Guinevere sipped a small glass of brandy and told him about Evelyn Pemberton.

"Trina said she sounds perfect. Types seventy-five words a minute and is very poised. I'm going to meet her tomorrow. If everything clicks, I'll send her over for you to interview the next day. How's that?"

Zac cradled her against his shoulder, his fingertips resting lightly over the small curve of her breast. "It's about time. What took you so long? You've got dozens of secretaries, who probably all want to go to work full time for a great employer like me."

"I wanted someone very special for you, Zac," she told him sweetly.

"I'll bet. A nice, robust, grandmotherly type, right? Has it taken you this long to find someone gray-haired and over fifty?"

34

Guinevere blinked. "Now, Zac . . ."

He grinned and pulled her closer. "It's all right. I understand completely. Besides, I've always had a thing for older women."

"Zachariah Justis!"

He tightened his grip as she indignantly tried to pull away. "Calm down. You didn't have to worry, you know. It wears me out just keeping up with you. I wouldn't have the energy to make it with my secretary even if she looked like a *Playboy* centerfold."

"Hah. That's what they all say."

To Guinevere's surprise, Zac took the remark seriously. "Who all says that? The guy who got off the elevator with you, maybe? I could see him having an affair with his secretary, while his wife waits at home. He looks the type."

In spite of Zac's enveloping warmth, a tiny shiver went through Guinevere. She suppressed it almost at once, but she was afraid Zac might have sensed it. "I was making a generalization," she said with a deliberate smile.

"Who is he?"

"The man on the elevator with me? His name is Rick Overstreet. I told you, he works at Gage and Watson. Want some more brandy?"

"No."

Zac hesitated and Guinevere held her breath, afraid he was going to ask more questions. But his strong, blunt fingers slipped inside the collar of her blouse instead.

"No," Zac repeated, his voice darkening, as he began to unbutton the blouse. "What I really want at the moment, is you."

Guinevere shivered again, but not from the tension connected with Rick Overstreet's name. This time it was strictly a result of the excitement that flared when Zac touched her.

"Zac," she whispered, eyes luminous, as he slipped the blouse off her shoulders.

"Come here," he murmured. "Give me something to think about besides my new secretary."

Guinevere sighed softly and went into his arms with the hot, exciting sense of abandon that always swept over her when Zac made love to her. Locked safely in his massive embrace, she gave herself wholeheartedly, rejoicing in the love that was growing steadily between them. She would let nothing interfere with this new love, Guinevere vowed silently. She would protect it and nurture it and care for it as if it were a delicate plant. She would let nothing come between herself and Zac.

The subject of Madame Zoltana came up spontaneously the next day during coffee break, when two of the women sharing the table with Guinevere and Francine Bates mentioned the psychic as they sat sipping their morning coffee. Guinevere was elated, because Zac had been singularly unhelpful in suggesting ways of steering the conversation in a specific direction. This was a stroke of luck, and it was the first break she'd had in her investigation. She tried to seize it without being too obvious.

"It's absolutely incredible, even if it is just clever guessing," confided Mary Hutchins. "I didn't believe anyone could really know that kind of stuff about a person's past, until Ruth introduced me to Madame

Zoltana. It was amazing. She knew about my husband's gallbladder operation. She told me Harold had just gotten a promotion, and could expect another one next year. She even knew that my mother-in-law was coming for a visit in the near future. Gives you the willies, when you think about it."

"Are you going back for another appointment?" Guinevere asked.

Mary hesitated. "I'm not sure. She told me last time she had to cut the session short because she was growing tired, but she promised me she could give me some helpful hints about decisions I'm going to have to make in the future, if I returned. The thing is, I don't really believe in this psychic nonsense, but this Madame Zoltana is—well, different than I expected. She really knows things. I'm not sure if I want to go back or not."

"What can it hurt, Mary?" Francine Bates asked logically. "You might learn something useful, something that could help you."

Ruth, the other woman at the table, bit her lip but said nothing. Guinevere wondered just exactly what Ruth had been told, and how often she was going to have to return to Madame Zoltana in order to keep her own personal secret from haunting her. Ruth reminded Guinevere a lot of Sally Evenson. There was that same fragile, uncertain air about both, as if they had been kicked in the teeth by life and were having a hard time recovering. Madame Zoltana was definitely not helping Sally, and Guinevere had a hunch she wasn't doing poor Ruth much good, either.

"I don't know," Mary Hutchins was saying. "I'm not sure I like this psychic business. Going once for a lark was fine, but I don't think I'll go back. It was a little spooky, if you want to know the truth." She looked at Guinevere. "What about you? Are you into the psychic bit?"

"I don't know," Guinevere said slowly, trying to sound convincingly uncertain. "I've never been to a psychic. It sounds fascinating, though." She turned to Ruth. "What do you think about this Madame Zoltana, Ruth?"

Ruth gnawed on her lower lip and studied the dregs of her coffee. "It's true," she said in a low voice. "She does see things, things she couldn't possibly know any other way except through her powers. And . . . and she tries to help."

"Help?" Guinevere prompted.

Ruth nodded slowly. "Sometimes she can use her power to . . . to change things just a little. Enough to keep them from hurting you." Ruth seemed to run out of words at that point. She lifted her head to look at Guinevere. "I don't know what to think, to tell you the truth. Would you like to meet her?"

Guinevere glanced at Francine Bates. "What do you think, Francine?"

"I went to her a couple of times. Nothing much came of it, but it was kind of fun. Like going to a gypsy fortune-teller at a fair or something. I didn't take it seriously."

"How much does it cost?" Guinevere asked.

"Just twenty dollars for one visit," Mary answered. "I guess it's worth it just for the experience. As I said, I'm not sure I'll go back, though."

"I think," Guinevere said carefully, "that I'd like to try it at least once. How do I set up an appointment?"

38

"That's easy," Mary assured her. "One of us who's already been to her can call and set it up. She only takes referrals, you know."

"That's interesting," said Guinevere. "The psychic business must be pretty good, if she can depend on making a living just on a referral basis."

"She doesn't want to be pestered by a bunch of skeptics trying to make fun of her power," Ruth explained in a small voice. "She doesn't mind people who are seriously interested, or even just curious, but she sees no need to waste her time with casual walk-ins. She says she's not a carnival sideshow and she doesn't want to be treated as one."

"I see," said Guinevere. "All right. I can't claim to be a believer, but I am genuinely curious. Go ahead and set up an appointment for me."

Chapter Three

The next day at Gage and Watson Guinevere deposited her shoulder bag in her desk drawer and went to work immediately. She had assigned herself this job in order to investigate Madame Zoltana, but that didn't mean she could stiff Gage and Watson. She had her professional ethics, and she would make certain the company got its money's worth from a Camelot Services employee. She was well into the document she was entering into the word processor, when Francine Bates arrived.

"Hey, it's all set, Gwen," the older woman announced lightly as she went to her desk. "I just saw Ruth and Mary in the hall. One of them made an appointment for you with Madame Zoltana. It's for this afternoon, right after work. I wrote down the address. It's a small house up on First Hill."

"I didn't know there were any houses left on First Hill," Guinevere said dryly. "I thought the hospitals had taken over most of the neighborhood." Several of Seattle's fine medical establishments had located in the district known as First Hill, an older area that looked out over the heart of the city toward Elliott Bay.

Francine laughed. "Not quite. There are a lot of apartments, and a few houses, still left."

"You said you'd only been to visit this Madame Zoltana once or twice, Francine?" Guinevere opened her drawer and stuffed the slip of paper with the address on it into her purse.

"That's all. I'm afraid I'm not a true believer. Or maybe I just don't want to believe, if you know what I mean." Francine paused thoughtfully as she started her word processor. Her voice grew more serious. "She really can tell you some incredible things. It can be . . . well, unsettling. But I think she helps some people."

"Helps them?"

Francine nodded. "Poor little Sally Evenson, who used to sit at the desk you're using, has really come to rely on her lately. Madame Zoltana has been a counselor and a sort of therapist for her."

Some therapist, Guinevere thought grimly. One who left the patient in a far worse condition than the one in which she'd found her. Whatever Zoltana's game with Sally had been, as far as Guinevere was concerned it was the next best thing to blackmail. "Well, I'll withhold judgment until I've met the woman," she told Francine, just as Miss Malcolm arrived.

Two hours later, at eleven o'clock, Guinevere got up from the word processor with a small sigh of relief. She forgot sometimes just how hard this kind of work could be. Coffee break was hailed joyously by one and all when it arrived.

"I'll see you down in the cafeteria," Guinevere said to Francine as they left the office and started down the hall. "I want to stop by the ladies' room first."

Francine nodded. "Okay. We'll be waiting."

Inside the rest room, Guinevere checked her hair, washed her hands, and straightened her royal blue blazer. A Camelot Services employee was supposed to look professional at all times. Satisfied, she went back out to the corridor, deciding to give Zac a ring. He was supposed to be meeting with the interior designer of his new office today for a final rundown on plans and preparations. Zac had not gotten along well with the interior designer during the past few weeks. There had been numerous arguments over what constituted essential furnishings and what nonessential furnishings. There had also been several knock-down-drag-out discussions over the cost of everything from the floor covering to the desk calendars. On most of those occasions only Guinevere's presence had forestalled all-out warfare. Unfortunately, she couldn't attend today's conference.

She was halfway down the hall en route to the pay phone at the other end, when Rich Overstreet glided out of his office and into her path. His movements were catlike, like his eyes. Guinevere, who had been doing her best to avoid any such accidental meetings, managed a polite smile.

"Good morning, Rick." She accompanied the greeting with a small nod and attempted to step past him.

"Join me for a cup of coffee, Gwen." Rick did not move out of her way. The golden cat's eyes were intent and serious. "It's been a long time."

"I'm afraid I can't just now. I have to make a phone call, and then I've got to meet some friends down in the cafeteria."

His mouth crooked sardonically. "Don't I qualify as a friend?"

42

Guinevere gave up any pretense of superficial politeness. Two years had not changed Rick Overstreet; you still had to be blunt to get through to him. "Not exactly, no."

He put out a hand and caught her arm, his fingers resting on the fabric of her blazer. "Gwen, you know that's not true. It's been two long years and everything's changed now."

She lifted her chin, her eyes scathing. "Because your wife is dead? That doesn't change a thing, Rick. Please let me go."

"Did I hurt you so badly two years ago?" he asked gently.

"No."

"I think you're lying, Gwen."

"I was never the one who lied, Rick. You were the one who had that bad habit."

He shrugged slightly. "Can you blame me? I wanted you very badly, Gwen. I knew you wouldn't come to me if you found out about Elena."

"You were right." She had found out about Elena, just before she had been about to leave on that first weekend trip with Rick. Guinevere had been horrified, hurt and infuriated. But she had been grateful she'd discovered the truth before she had gone to bed with Rick Overstreet. The thought of being the other woman made her sick.

His eyes warmed with masculine promise. "Elena's gone now."

"So is whatever we once had," Guinevere said heartily. "Please let go of my arm, Rick."

"How long have you been seeing that guy who met

you for lunch yesterday? He looked, as if he owned you."

Guinevere's eyes narrowed. "No one owns me, Rick. You of all people should know that."

Rick ignored the crack. "He didn't look like your type at all, Gwen."

"You're hardly an authority."

"More of an authority than you want to admit, and you know it," he said softly, his fingers still gripping her sleeve. "We could have been good together, Gwen, if you hadn't lost your nerve."

"It was hardly a question of losing my nerve. What I lost was my faith in you. You were a lying, cheating bastard then, Rick, and I doubt you've changed one bit. Excuse me." She jerked free of his grip and strode briskly down the hall, not looking back. What rotten luck to run into him here at Gage and Watson after all this time. One of the perils of being an undercover investigator, Guinevere told herself with an inner sigh.

Zac answered the phone on the third ring. Guinevere knew at once that things were not going well on the other end.

"I hope you're not yelling at her again, Zac. If you're not careful she's going to abandon the whole job before you move in, and then where will you be?"

"Not much worse off, if you ask me. Do you know what she wants to do now, Gwen? She wants to put grass on one entire wall. *Grass,* of all things. She's gone crazy."

"I expect she's talking about grass cloth, Zac. It makes a very handsome wall covering."

"There's already a nice coat of paint on all the walls."

"Yes, but having one wall papered will soften the overall effect. Trust her, Zac. You hired her for her advice, so take it. Listen, I called to tell you I've got my big break in the Zoltana case," she went on excitedly.

"I'm not sure if I can stand the suspense."

"Now, Zac, don't be condescending. This is important. I'm going to have my first appointment with Madame Zoltana tonight after work."

"Ask her to look into her crystal ball and tell you whether this interior designer of mine is going to survive until the end of the week, or if I'll be charged with justifiable homicide."

"You aren't taking this seriously, are you?"

"Damn right, I'm taking it seriously. Between you and the interior designer, the assets of Free Enterprise Security are going to be wiped out before I ever get into my new office."

"I mean my case. You're not taking my case seriously."

"You want me to get on your case?" he threatened mildly.

"Not particularly," she retorted. "All right, Zac, go back to sniping at your interior designer. I've got more important things to do. I just thought I'd let you know where I'll be after work, since you said something about having dinner together this evening."

"I'll be at your place when you get home. Don't be late, or I'll eat without you." Zak broke off to yell at the hapless designer. "For God's sake," Guinevere heard him shout, "put away that damn baby blue. I am not having baby blue in my new office."

"I'll see you for dinner," Guinevere said into the

phone. "You can cook." She hung up the phone before Zac could respond, wondering what he would end up bringing home for dinner. He was spending a great deal of time at her apartment these days, moving in slowly but surely, as if he hoped she wouldn't notice. A couple of his shirts were now hanging unobtrusively in her closet, and he kept a toothbrush in the bathroom. His socks and underwear were starting to show up in a dresser drawer, all carefully folded. At least he was neat.

Guinevere smiled to herself at the thought of Zac trying to be subtle. She left the pay phone and started toward the elevators. It was as she pressed the call button that she glanced back and saw Rick Overstreet leaning casually in the doorway of his office, lighting one of his fancy cigarettes. His eyes never left her as she got into the elevator. Guinevere shuddered as the elevator doors slid shut. He was beginning to make her feel like prey, she realized. And she hated the sensation.

At lunchtime she hurried back to Camelot Services to conduct the interview with Evelyn Pemberton. Trina smiled knowingly as the secretarial candidate walked through the door, and Guinevere had to smile back. Miss Pemberton appeared at first glance to be exactly what she had been waiting for. In her early fifties, the handsome, gray-haired woman wore her years and experience with a womanly authority that Guinevere responded to at once. She'd like to have that same confident authority when she reached Miss Pemberton's age. Guinevere rose to greet her, giving the woman her most charming smile.

"How do you do, Miss Pemberton. Please sit down.

I'm so glad you could come. Miss Hood has explained the job to you?"

"She gave me an overview when I talked to her." Evelyn Pemberton nodded cordially at Trina, who was getting ready to leave for lunch. "Mr. Justis sounds as if he can be a bit of a handful at times, but I've been married for twenty-five years and raised two sons. I'm quite familiar with the male of the species. They have their occasional ego problems, and they can be temperamental, but I've learned to manage over the years."

Guinevere nodded in enthusiastic agreement. "Mr. Justis needs someone who can maintain a calm office environment. His clients are often nervous and worried, as you can imagine. It's the nature of his business, of course. During the past year, his client list has been growing quite steadily, and he's reached the point where he needs full-time secretarial assistance. The job routines will be quite varied, and confidentiality is an absolute must." Guinevere glanced shrewdly at Evelyn Pemberton. "You do understand that? Mr. Justis would let you go in an instant if he thought you had been indiscreet about one of his cases." But first, Guinevere added silently, he'd probably chew you to pieces.

"And he'd probably chew me up into little bits before he fired me, right?" Evelyn Pemberton asked easily.

Guinevere grinned. "I think, Miss Pemberton, that you have a good grasp of the job requirements. I'll send you over to talk to Mr. Justis first thing in the morning."

"That will be fine."

* * *

Guinevere found the little house on First Hill without too much trouble. It was located in the shade of an old brick apartment building that filled up most of the rest of the block. Madame Zoltana apparently did not believe in advertising. There was no sign out front announcing the sort of service being offered inside. The house was a basic, old-fashioned frame structure with a well-tended garden stretching around to the back. The curtains in the windows were dark and heavy and pulled shut, which was surprising on such a pleasant, sunny day.

There was nothing to announce that this was the abode of a rip-off psychic. Guinevere checked the address one more time before going up the front porch steps. As she lifted her hand to knock on the screen door, it occurred to her that she was nervous. She had a fleeting wish that Zac had accompanied her, and instantly gave herself a mental kick for being so chicken. This was her case, not his.

The door was opened on the second knock, and Guinevere found herself facing a bosomy woman in her late fifties. Her face was serenely austere, almost aristocratic. Piercing blue eyes regarded Guinevere with cool inquiry. The woman was dressed in a black caftan trimmed at hem and sleeve with a white, embroidered design. Her hair was silvered and worn very long. It fell down her back in soft waves. Several silver bracelets and necklaces jangled lightly when she moved. A cigarette dangled carelessly from her right hand. The room behind her was quite dark, due to the drawn curtains, and smelled of stale cigarette smoke, and Guinevere could see very little in the darkness.

"Madame Zoltana?"

The woman inclined her head regally. "I am she. What can I do for you?"

"I'm Guinevere Jones. I have an appointment with you." Guinevere was still fighting a strange sense of nervousness. Planning the big exposé of Madame Zoltana's shady business practices was one thing; carrying out those plans was clearly going to be another. For some reason, Madame Zoltana wasn't quite what she had expected. There was too much shrewd intelligence in those blue eyes, and an unnerving degree of quiet arrogance in Madame Zoltana's posture. It occurred to Guinevere that she might have bitten off more than she could chew. Instantly she pushed aside the notion and summoned up one of her famous, charming smiles—the kind of smile Zac claimed made people want to instantly confide their most secret thoughts. Madame Zoltana did not respond to the smile.

"Come in," the woman said coolly, standing aside.

Guinevere took a few steps into the darkened room, and as her eyes grew accustomed to the shadows, she glanced around at the simple, old-fashioned over-stuffed furniture, which appeared to date from the forties, as did the house itself. Several overflowing ash-trays were scattered around. On one side of the room an arched opening revealed a small dining alcove, and on the other side a doorway opened onto a dark hall that apparently led to the bedrooms.

"My contemplation room is through here," Madame Zoltana said quietly, moving past Guinevere soundlessly.

Guinevere followed her into the dim hall and

through a doorway that opened onto a small carpeted and heavily draped chamber. The only furniture here was a round table and two chairs. The walls were painted a dark gray, giving the whole room a cloudy appearance. In the center of the table was a thick crystal dish in the shape of a large salad bowl. Not the traditional crystal ball, Guinevere thought disparagingly.

"Please sit down." Madame Zoltana lowered herself into one of the chairs and waited until Guinevere was seated. She looked at her client over the top of the crystal bowl. "You are not a believer."

"No," Guinevere said, opting for honesty. "But I am interested and curious. I'm also open-minded. I've never met a psychic. My friends at work tell me you're quite genuine. I wanted to see for myself."

Madame Zoltana continued to stare, her blue eyes riveting in their intensity. "I accept that your interest is genuine. You must understand that I do not normally like to waste my time trying to convince skeptics. I have too many other important things to do. I can only see a limited number of clients. The sessions are very tiring for me, and it takes several hours to renew my energies after a client has left."

"I understand."

"My fees have been explained to you?"

That's right, Guinevere thought grimly, get the money settled first. "Of course." She reached into her purse and removed a twenty-dollar bill from her wallet. "Will this cover the session?"

"Yes." Madame Zoltana took the money. It vanished into a caftan pocket. She leaned forward, cradling the heavy crystal bowl between her hands. There was a long silence, and then Zoltana said, "You are here only to explore the matter of psychic powers. Therefore I will not attempt to read the future for you. It requires much effort, and in this case it does not seem to be worth it. You probably wouldn't believe what I had to tell you anyway. But perhaps I can satisfy your intellectual interest with some observations about you and your past."

"Why do you use a bowl?"

"Instead of a crystal ball, you mean?" Madame Zoltana smiled thinly. "It doesn't matter what shape the crystal takes, so long as it is of the best quality. Crystal has curious properties. It enables one to focus more easily. It is possible to work without the aid of crystal, but much more difficult. What really makes the difference is having the Gift. Without it, it wouldn't matter how much crystal one used. Seeing through the veils of the past and the future would be impossible."

"And you have the Gift?" Guinevere was careful to keep the question sincere.

Madame Zoltana inclined her head. "It is both a blessing and a curse." She stubbed out her cigarette in a nearby ashtray.

Just like running any small business, Guinevere thought wryly. A blessing and a curse. She wondered how Zoltana listed her occupation with the IRS.

Guinevere waited as Madame Zoltana composed herself and stared into the crystal bowl. There was another long period of silence, during which Guinevere felt her palms grow moist again. Zac would laugh at her if he knew how anxious she felt at the moment.

Surreptitiously she dried her palms on her skirt, and waited.

At first Guinevere thought the room was growing marginally darker, then she realized that the bowl in the center of the table seemed to be glowing very faintly. Probably her imagination, she told herself. Either that, or some lighting trick. No telling what gadgets were concealed under or in the table.

Finally Madame Zoltana began to speak. The words came out faintly, with what sounded like a great deal of effort. Guinevere leaned forward to hear clearly.

"I see many things," Madame Zoltana whispered. "Some are insignificant. You are not married. You live alone, although there is a man who shares more and more of your life these days. You have a younger sister, a very beautiful sister, who has at times been a trial to you. You work in an office, using a typing machine of some sort, but you aren't a secretary or clerk." Madame Zoltana frowned. "I don't understand. . . . Ah, yes, it becomes clear. You own your own business, one that involves secretaries and clerks and various other kinds of office personnel. At times, you, too, do such work."

Guinevere was startled, by the references both to Carla and to the fact that she herself wasn't just an employee of Camelot Services. This woman had definitely done some research. Guinevere kept her mouth shut, waiting for Madame Zoltana to continue.

"You are thirty years old. This man with whom you are presently involved is somewhat older, perhaps in his mid thirties." Zoltana's brow wrinkled slightly. "But even though he is only a few years older than you, in some ways he is much older. He has perhaps seen too much of some things in life. Perhaps this is why he needs you. He is very strong in many ways." Zoltana hesitated and her brow relaxed. "Ah, yes, he is a good lover."

Guinevere flushed in spite of herself. She would have to remember to mention that last observation to Zac.

Madame Zoltana fell silent for a few minutes, and Guinevere began to wonder if the session was already over. But the psychic did not look up from the faintly glowing bowl. She appeared to be contemplating something she saw in the crystal depths. "There is something more that has to do with this man, but it is not clear. I told you that I would not put myself to the effort of reading the future for you, but I am getting hints of it. I cannot ignore them. Do you wish me to look forward?" Madame Zoltana did not raise her head.

"How much?" Guinevere asked dryly.

"Another twenty dollars."

She would consider it as expenses having to do with the investigation, Guinevere decided. Zac always kept a precise expense account when he was working. She reached into her wallet and withdrew another twenty. "All right. Tell me what you see."

"It has to do with this man in your life. There are indications of danger." Zoltana hesitated again. "I cannot tell if the danger is aimed at him or emanates from him. Perhaps both." Another tense pause. "I see fear in you. Fear of this man you love. There is a threat, and you do not know how to deal with it. You, too, are in danger. You must be very, very careful, because when the moment of truth arrives you will not be certain you can trust this man."

Guinevere realized she was holding her breath. The nervousness she had been experiencing was now tinged with dread. She forced herself to take a calming breath, reminding herself that creating this kind of vague fear was Madame Zoltana's stock in trade. Guinevere had to admit the woman was surprisingly good at it. Angry at her own unexpected gullibility, Guinevere tried to shake off the uneasy sensation that was enveloping her. She waited tensely for Madame Zoltana to continue. The psychic continued to stare into the crystal bowl, her forehead lined again with concentration, but eventually she sighed and sat back, breaking the spell. Her blue eyes were fixed on Guinevere's face.

"I can tell you no more today. I am at the limit of my abilities. If you wish to know more, you must return at another time. Please go now. I must rest."

Madame Zoltana got to her feet, steadying herself with a hand on the back of her chair. Reaching for a cigarette, she waited for Guinevere to precede her out of the room.

With a last glance at the crystal bowl, Guinevere obeyed the woman's instructions to leave. At the doorway, she looked back once more, trying to decide if the bowl had really glowed for a few moments. She still couldn't be certain.

As soon as she stepped outside into the warm summer day, Guinevere managed to forget much of the odd sensation that had gripped her during those tense moments inside the house. The power of suggestion really was quite amazing, she marveled as she hurried toward her compact, parked at the curb. She couldn't wait to tell Zac.

Zac was aware of a comfortable, homey feeling as he heard Guinevere's key in the lock. He put down the knife he was using to slice tomatoes, picked up his glass of tequila and the glass of wine he had poured for Guinevere, and went to meet her. She came through the door looking mildly disheveled and more concerned than he had expected. He bent his head to give her a short, forceful kiss and handed her the wine.

"Hey, what happened? Madame Zoltana get to you after all? The woman must be a real pro."

Guinevere took a grateful swallow of wine and held up the glass. "Thanks, I needed that. Madame Zoltana was a strange experience, Zac. Not quite what I was expecting." She sniffed appreciatively. "What's cooking?"

"I'm glad to see the experience didn't manage to spoil your appetite. I'm making tacos." He turned back toward the kitchen and Guinevere followed, tossing her purse into a hall closet en route. He set his tequila back down on the counter and picked up the knife. "So tell me all about it. How's the big-time psychic investigation going?"

Guinevere sat on a kitchen stool, one leg swinging idly over the other as she sipped her wine and watched Zac prepare the taco fillings. "Well, for openers, she told me right away I didn't just work as a temporary secretary. She knew I owned Camelot Services, Zac."

"Is that so?" He was amused, but he kept a serious expression on his face as he grated cheese. "Anything else?"

"She knew about Carla. Knew she was beautiful and that she's occasionally been a pain in the ass."

"Uh-huh. What else?"

He thought Guinevere hesitated a long time before she continued. It was obvious she had been slightly disconcerted by her experience. "She mentioned a man in my life," Guinevere said slowly. "I'm sure it was you. She seemed to know something about you."

"What, exactly?" Zac asked sardonically as he picked up his glass of tequila.

"She mentioned danger around you, for one thing."

"Must have guessed I was going to be slicing tomatoes tonight. I've been known to cut myself with a sharp knife while slicing tomatoes. Anything else?"

Again Guinevere paused. "No, not really."

"How much did this little investigation set you back?"

"Forty bucks," Guinevere said, grimacing.

"And, of course, if you want to know the good stuff, you'll have to go back."

"Precisely. Madame Zoltana exhausts herself easily."

Zac leaned back against the counter, taking pity on her, she seemed so serious. "What's the problem, Gwen? You knew she was a con artist."

"Well, yes. But she did seem to know things, Zac. I was very careful about what I said around Gage and Watson. I don't see how some of that information could have gotten back to her."

"Sounds to me as if she just had someone take a look inside your purse."

Guinevere's eyes opened wide. "My purse!"

Zac's mouth curved faintly. "Follow me." He saun-

tered back into the hall, opened the closet, and removed Guinevere's shoulder bag. He unzipped it and
turned it upside down, emptying the contents onto a
small table. Tossing aside the leather purse, he pushed
his fingers idly through the motley collection.

"Here we go, a business card with *Camelot Services*
stamped on it in nice big letters, and you listed as
president. Your driver's license, identifying you as
Guinevere Jones, the same name as the president of
Camelot Services. It also tells us several other things
about you, including the fact that you are thirty years
old." He flicked through a few other items. "A note to
call Carla. A photo of Carla standing outside her new
art gallery, and an announcement of the opening of
the gallery. Carla's last name is the same as your last
name. It wouldn't take much guesswork to figure out
she's your sister, and everyone knows younger sisters
are occasionally pains in the ass, especially when
they're good-looking. It's all here, Gwen. Everything
Madame Zoltana revealed to you was revealed to her
first by someone who went through your purse."

"You're absolutely right," Guinevere breathed.
"That explains everything. It also fits with my theory
of her having an inside person at Gage and Watson. I
left my purse in my desk drawer several times yesterday, and again today. It would have been very easy for
someone to have a look through it."

"Yeah."

"But what about you, Zac? She knew about you
too."

He grinned. "What did she know about me? Use
your head, Gwen. Whoever works for her at G and W
probably saw you meet me for lunch yesterday. It

wouldn't have taken any great psychic power to figure out that you and I are seeing each other for some nonplatonic reasons." Especially not after the way you kissed me in front of that turkey who was trying to make a pass at you as you got off the elevator, Zac added to himself.

"What about the danger she hinted at?"

"That was the hook, the bait to make you return for a few more visits. Vague references to danger are probably standard operating procedure for her. By the next time she would have learned even more about you."

Guinevere's mood lightened several degrees as she assimilated his logic. "Yes, it all makes sense. What a racket. The thing is, Zac, she's really very good. She creates this odd atmosphere that is very convincing."

"Good con artists are all very convincing. They have to be, in order to make a living. Ready to eat?"

"Mmm-hmm." Guinevere followed him back through the kitchen door, wondering why she hadn't told him everything Madame Zoltana had said. For some reason she didn't want to examine too closely, Guinevere didn't want to bring up the fact that Zoltana had warned her she would soon feel fear around Zac. And Guinevere didn't want to think about the other warning, the one that implied she might not be able to trust Zac when the chips were down. The problem was, she had let Zoltana get to her, allowed the woman to prey on her imagination. Gullible Guinevere.

"You know, Zac," she said as she set the table, "you look cute in an apron."

Chapter Four

It was touching, Zac decided the next day as he interviewed Evelyn Pemberton, really touching. When he thought of how hard Guinevere must have worked to avoid sending him a bright-eyed, sexy little ex-cheerleader, he got a nice warm feeling deep inside. Somewhere in the vicinity below his belt, to be precise. The notion of Guinevere going out of her way to make certain he wouldn't be put in any danger of being seduced by a sweet young thing amused him no end. After all her hard work, he almost hated to have to tell her that Evelyn Pemberton was exactly what he'd had in mind from the beginning.

Already he was beginning to relax around Mrs. Pemberton. No doubt about it, the woman inspired confidence. He could envision her already seated at the desk in the outer office of the new suite upstairs, organizing the daily business and calming clients. The fact that she could type was simply an added bonus, as far as Zac was concerned. He couldn't wait to put everything in her hands.

"Mrs. Pemberton, I think this is going to work out beautifully," he announced with satisfaction after only fifteen minutes of interviewing. "Free Enterprise Security will be moving upstairs to its new offices on the twentieth. I'd like you to start on that date. Now, Gwen tells me there are some tax forms we have to fill out." He scrabbled around in a desk drawer trying to find them as he spoke. "And I think we have to file something with Social Security, too. I'm not exactly sure what, but Gwen will know." He looked up hopefully. "Or perhaps you know the routine?"

She smiled benignly at his blatant relief and enthusiasm. "I know the routine, Mr. Justis," she said gently, "but I don't think we're quite ready for it yet."

He stared at her blankly. "Not ready?"

"Mr. Justis, I assure you the opening you have sounds very interesting, and I will give it my closest consideration, but I really must have a few days to think about it. And I'm sure you'll want to interview other people."

"Uh, no, I don't," he said flatly, stunned by this turn of events. "I'm offering you the job."

"Well, I certainly appreciate it. I'll let you know my decision next week."

"Next week?" he repeated. "Next *week?*"

"Yes. At that time, if I decide to accept your offer, we can discuss the pension plan you're offering." She rose to leave, a graceful woman who moved with confidence. "Good-bye, Mr. Justis. I'll call you as soon as I've made my decision."

Zac stared after her, stricken. The closing of the door jolted him out of his trance. He grabbed the phone and dialed the number of Camelot Services. When Trina answered he didn't even give her time to finish the greeting.

"Put Gwen on the phone," Zac ordered. "Now."

"I'm sorry, Zac, I can't do that. She's at Gage and Watson."

"Oh, hell, that's right." He glanced irritably at his watch. "Then call Gage and Watson and tell her I want to talk to her immediately."

"What's the matter, Zac? Didn't Evelyn Pemberton work out?"

"Just get hold of Gwen. Tell her she's got a very unhappy client on her hands. Namely, me." He dropped the receiver into the cradle and waited for Gwen to call, drumming his fingers on the desk. It took ten long minutes. When the instrument did ring he snatched it up.

"Zac? What's wrong? Trina said you sounded upset."

"You told me Evelyn Pemberton was mine if I wanted her."

"She is."

"Well, I want her, and she doesn't seem to want me. What the hell went wrong? I thought you knew what you were doing when it came to this sort of thing. Lord knows, I waited long enough to get even one potential candidate out of you. Now the candidate tells me she'll think about the offer and get back to me next week sometime. Furthermore, if she does decide to take the job, she made it clear she wants to know about my pension plan. Gwen, I haven't *got* a pension plan."

"Is that all? Zac, she's a pro. She's going to make you cool your heels a bit so you'll appreciate her all the more when she agrees to take the job. Don't worry, she'll say yes when she calls."

"Christ, you'd think I was asking her to marry me!"

"She's not being coy, she's being businesslike. Trust me, Zac."

"You keep saying that," he complained. "What about my nonexistent pension plan?"

"I know what I'm doing. And I'll put you in touch with the people who can help you set up a small pension plan. Now stop worrying. Listen, I was going to call you anyway. Meet me for lunch, okay? I want to consult."

"Consult about what?" Then it clicked. "Oh, yeah, your big case."

"Why is it I keep getting the impression you're not taking my big case seriously?"

"I am taking it seriously. I think it's a complete and utter waste of your time and money, but I'm taking it seriously."

"Sure." She didn't sound mollified. "All right, pick me up for lunch at noon. I'll meet you in the lobby of the building."

"Okay. Listen, Gwen, are you sure about Evelyn Pemberton?"

"Trust me, Zac."

Zac hung up with a groan and sat glaring for a few minutes at the two Mason Adair paintings he had hanging on the walls of his tiny office. For a moment he simply stared at them. Then he thought about Gwen and her big case, and a reluctant smile curved the edges of his mouth. He was beginning to enjoy her Nancy Drew enthusiasm. There were a lot of things he enjoyed about Guinevere Jones.

Guinevere was all business as she sat down to lunch with Zac in a small deli between First and Western

Avenues. "I've been thinking all morning about what you said last night," she began, watching him bite into a huge sandwich.

"Nice to know you're hanging on my every word."

"About my purse," she reminded him. "Zac, please pay attention. I'm trying to consult with you."

"My usual consulting fee is two hundred dollars an hour."

"How about I pay for lunch?"

"It's a deal." He glanced at his watch. "You've got fifty minutes left."

Guinevere considered giving him a swift kick under the table but decided against it. She realized Zac was finding her current efforts amusing, but that didn't mean she couldn't pick his brain—if she could just keep his attention from wandering. She leaned forward intently.

"I think you're right about someone having gone through my purse, reporting certain details to Madame Zoltana before my appointment last night."

"I know I'm right." He took another satisfying bite of his sandwich.

"I've done some observation this morning, and the way I figure it, there aren't too many people who would have had access to my purse. The most likely suspect is Francine Bates and she's the one who originally turned Sally on to Madame Zoltana. Francine has this nice, motherly sort of personality. I can just see Sally confiding in her about the baby and everything."

"Have you got any evidence against Francine?"

"Nope. So I've decided to set a trap."

Zac chewed thoughtfully for a moment before repeating cautiously, "A trap?"

"That's right. I want to see what you think of my idea." Guinevere sat back and smiled brilliantly.

He sighed. "Go ahead. It's your hour."

"Here's what I'm going to do. I'm going to give Francine some exciting little tidbit and make sure that no one besides her knows about it. Then I'll see if Madame Zoltana mentions it at the next session."

"Hmm. When's the next session?"

"I'm going to call Zoltana this afternoon and set it up as soon as possible."

Zac finished the first half of his sandwich. "What's the tidbit you're going to give Francine?"

"Oh, I thought I'd tell her I'm worrying about my brother going back to jail," Guinevere said airily.

"You don't have a brother."

"That's the whole point, Zac. When that false bit of information crops up during a session, I'll know for sure that Francine was the one who planted it. Then I'll have proof that she and Zoltana are working together."

Zac shook his head and reached for the other half of his sandwich. "The only one you'll prove anything to is yourself. Zoltana's clients probably won't believe you."

"Well, I can certainly make a scene at Gage and Watson, and most of the doubters will believe me."

"Does it occur to you that Madame Zoltana and her cohort aren't going to be thrilled when you start accusing them of conspiracy?"

"What can they do about it?"

"Sue you for slander," Zac suggested mildly.

Guinevere frowned. "Nonsense. I'll be telling the truth."

"It's going to be your word against theirs," he pointed out.

"Well, at the very least, I'm going to make sure Sally Evenson knows the truth. Besides, someone like Zoltana is not about to sue. She'd have to prove her powers are for real, and she couldn't do that."

"Just keep telling yourself that, when you find yourself hiring a lawyer."

"Don't try to alarm me, Zac."

"Okay. Is the consultation over?"

"I guess so," Guinevere said reluctantly. "Although you haven't exactly been a big help."

"Consultants get paid whether they're a big help or not. It's one of the joys of consulting work. Now, if you're finished, you can tell me how the hell I'm supposed to set up a pension plan for a single employee."

Guinevere grinned. "That kind of consulting will cost you lunch tomorrow."

"You're a hard woman, Guinevere Jones."

"It's the company I've been keeping lately," she explained.

Guinevere planted her false tidbit with great care right after lunch. She walked back into the office with her head bent over a letter she held in her hand, making sure her expression was troubled, and when she sat down beside Francine Bates she didn't give her the usual friendly greeting.

Francine watched for a while as Guinevere made a show of concentrating intently on her work. Finally the older woman spoke.

"Everything okay, Gwen? You look worried."

Guinevere sniffed slightly and reached for a tissue. "I'm fine," she said through a bleak smile as she dabbed delicately at her nose. She'd never done any acting. Warning herself not to overplay the part, she added wearily, "Family problems. You know how it is."

"That's for sure," Francine said consolingly. "Sometimes it helps to talk about it, though."

"I wouldn't want to burden you with my personal problems," Guinevere said bravely, stuffing the tissue back into her purse.

"I don't mind, Gwen. What are friends for?"

After that it was easy. During the afternoon coffee break, Guinevere allowed Francine to coax the whole sordid story out of her.

"We all thought he was doing so well," she concluded dismally. "My parents had such hopes, and now he goes and gets himself arrested again. Oh, he claims he's innocent, of course, but who's going to believe him, with his record? If only he hadn't gone to Los Angeles."

"Just another young kid drawn by the bright lights of Southern California," Francine said sadly. "Happens all the time. How is the rest of the family coping?"

"About as you'd expect. My mother is heartbroken. Dad is disgusted. I'm not sure he's going to be willing to hire a lawyer this time."

"What an awful situation."

"If only I knew what to do, and what was going to happen next." Guinevere summoned a shaky smile. "I'm half thinking about going back to Madame

Zoltana's. I'm not sure I believe in her powers, but I honestly don't know where else to turn."

"Why not?" Francine agreed gently. "She might be able to give you a little hope, and we all need that from time to time."

"I think I'll give her a call before we go back to work," Guinevere said with sudden conviction.

But there was no answer when Guinevere dialed Madame Zoltana's number. She waited impatiently another hour and then slipped out of the office to try calling again.

"Any luck?" Francine asked when Guinevere returned from the second attempt.

"No. I guess she's out for the day."

"Maybe you'll be able to reach her this evening."

"Maybe."

But Guinevere couldn't get hold of Madame Zoltana that evening either. It was very frustrating, and she told Zac as much when he showed up at her door after work.

"My big plan is going down the tubes, Zac. Why isn't she answering her phone? I was all set to see her again today after I left Gage and Watson."

"Who knows? Maybe she's taken a temporary vacation on another astral plane." Zac wandered into the kitchen to see what Guinevere had going for dinner.

"I do wish you'd stop making jokes about this case, Zac," she muttered as she followed him into the bright yellow kitchen.

"You never want me to have any fun," he observed as he reached for the tequila bottle in her cupboard.

Guinevere mumbled something under her breath.

"Did you mention earlier that you were inviting yourself for dinner this evening?" she asked meaningfully.

"I don't believe I did. When I left the office my feet just sort of naturally turned in this direction." He poured the tequila and recapped the bottle. "Did you make enough for two?"

Guinevere grinned. "Luckily for you I just sort of naturally bought enough shrimp for two."

"I think I begin to see a pattern developing in our lives," Zac said with a certain satisfaction.

Guinevere had no more luck getting hold of the elusive Zoltana the following morning. She was becoming increasingly frustrated, but she forgot some of her irritation when Francine Bates showed up late for work. For the first time since she had met Francine, the older woman was not cheerful or friendly. She seemed withdrawn and preoccupied. Guinevere began to wonder if perhaps Francine and Madame Zoltana had put two and two together and decided they were being set up by one Guinevere Jones.

"I think my cover may be blown," Guinevere confided to Zac at lunchtime. "Francine hasn't said two words to me all day, and I can't get hold of Madame Zoltana. Do you think they might have become suspicious when they discovered I was really the owner of Camelot Services, and not just another employee?"

"I don't see why. As far as they know, you were just filling in for one of your employees and didn't want to have everyone know you owned the firm," Zac reassured her.

"Well, what do I do now?"

Zac shrugged. "You could see if anyone else has had

any better luck getting an appointment with Zoltana. If someone else has, you can assume Zoltana's probably avoiding you."

Guinevere brightened. "That's an excellent idea, Zac. Sometimes you're positively brilliant."

"I know," he said modestly.

She went back to Gage and Watson determined to track down Mary and Ruth. Mary hadn't tried to get hold of Madame Zoltana, but Ruth had made an effort three times the previous day and had failed. She seemed very depressed about the situation.

"I don't know what to do," she confided to Guinevere. "I've got to talk to her. I'm going crazy with worry. She always seems to know what's happening, and she's been keeping things under control for me. I know you might not believe it, but it's true. Now I can't reach her, and I'm frantic."

On a hunch, Guinevere tried Sally Evenson next. Sally seemed happy enough in her new temporary assignment, but when Guinevere asked her about Madame Zoltana, she didn't sound quite so cheerful.

"I have an appointment with her after work this afternoon, Miss Jones. I know you think I shouldn't go, but I *have* to go."

"I understand, Sally. Look, do me a favor and call me after you've seen her, all right? I want to talk to you about the session."

"Well, all right."

But when Sally phoned Guinevere at home that evening, her voice sounded odd, as if she was half relieved, half terrified. "There was no one home, Miss Jones. I went to her house just like I always do, and she wasn't there. What do you think it means? Maybe she isn't going to help me anymore."

"Sally, listen to me. Madame Zoltana wasn't helping you to begin with. She has no more psychic power than I do. You've just saved twenty bucks."

"Thirty," Sally said almost inaudibly.

"Thirty!"

"That's what I've been paying lately, ever since she said she could keep things under control for me. Oh, Miss Jones, I don't know what to do!"

Guinevere glanced through the kitchen door at Zac, who had his feet up on her coffee table while he read the evening paper. He seemed to be ignoring the conversation. "Sally, you're an adult woman with a good job. You have your own life under control. You don't need anyone else to control it for you. Now, tell me how you like your new assignment."

They talked for a few more minutes, and Guinevere tried to find lots of encouraging things to say. When they hung up she went thoughtfully out into the living room, plunking herself down beside Zac on the sofa.

"You know what I think?" she demanded.

"What?" He looked up from the newspaper.

"I think Madame Zoltana is lying low."

"You could be right. But I'm not quite sure why she would bother. To be honest, Gwen, you aren't much of a threat."

"Hah! I'll bet Madame Zoltana thinks I am," Guinevere said with some satisfaction. "Let me have the comics." She reached for a section of the paper. "I think I'll drive by Madame Zoltana's tomorrow and see if she's at home."

"Waste of time," Zac promised.

Zac was right, Guinevere had to admit the next day after work when she parked in front of Madame Zoltana's little house. There was no sign of Madame Zoltana. All the drapes were still pulled, so she couldn't peer through the windows, but after she'd knocked loudly several times, Guinevere was sure no one was home.

She walked back down the front path to the sidewalk and glanced around at the neighborhood. The only real neighbors lived in the big brick apartment house that filled up the block. They weren't likely to have noted the actions of the local psychic who lived in the little house on the corner. Guinevere decided she could hardly just start knocking on apartment doors and asking questions. People would think she was nuts.

The following day, Francine Bates failed to show up for work. Guinevere was on the phone to Zac by noon.

"She's not here, Zac. Miss Malcolm says she hasn't phoned in sick or made any excuses. She simply didn't show up. That's very unusual behavior for Francine, according to everyone else in the office. I tried calling her at home, and there's no answer. And no one has been able to get hold of Madame Zoltana either. Zac, this is getting very mysterious."

"Not nearly as mysterious as these forms I'm supposed to fill out for an employee pension plan. What have you gotten me into, Gwen?"

"Zac, your attention is wandering. We are discussing my case."

"My professional opinion is that at the moment,

you don't have a case. Just as well. You weren't getting paid for solving it, anyway. Now, about these forms . . ."

Guinevere sighed and gave up. Zac was right. It was beginning to look as though she didn't have a case. She got off the phone after telling Zac to call his accountant about the pension plan forms, and went back down the hall, ignoring Rick Overstreet as she passed him lounging in an office doorway.

"You think that's going to work forever?" Rick asked softly as she swept by. "You can't pretend I don't exist, Gwen, and you know it."

Damned if she would give him the benefit of an answer or let him know how much she resented his predatory gaze. With a woman's intuition, she sensed that she was rapidly becoming a challenge for him. If they had never run into each other again, Guinevere was certain Rick Overstreet wouldn't have thought twice about her. But now fate had thrown her back into his path, and all of his egotistical machismo was aroused. Once he'd been able to charm her with ease. Apparently it annoyed him that he'd lost his touch.

All things considered, it seemed time to throw in the towel on this assignment. It was getting hard to avoid Rick Overstreet, and her big case seemed to have disintegrated. Guinevere decided she would send Sally Evenson back to Gage and Watson in the morning.

"A wise decision," Zac said that afternoon when she told him. "I've been saying all along that you were wasting your time."

"I know," Guinevere admitted, "but it's all very disappointing. My big case has disappeared."

"Don't worry, I'll make it up to you," Zac promised with a wicked grin. "By tomorrow morning you'll have forgotten the whole thing."

"Promises, promises."

"Trust me," said Zac.

Guinevere went back to business as usual at Camelot Services for the remainder of the week, but she kept tabs on Sally Evenson. By Friday Sally seemed much happier.

"At first I was worried about what I would do without Madame Zoltana's guidance," she confided to Guinevere. "But now I feel much better. It's a relief not to have to go for those appointments. I'm not worrying the way I did when she was always telling me things that made me nervous. I talked to my friend Ruth today, and she says she's feeling better too."

"Keep that in mind if Zoltana ever turns up again," Guinevere advised her. "You're much happier without her guidance. Did Francine Bates ever come back to work?"

"No, and it's very strange, really. No one can figure out what's happened to her. Miss Malcolm says she had Personnel make some inquiries, and they can't find her either."

Guinevere thought about that. She was grateful for the fact that Sally, at least, seemed to be much more cheerful.

Sally Evenson's cheerfulness vanished on the following Monday. She showed up at Camelot Services during her lunch hour, looking stricken. After one startled glance Guinevere and Trina rushed to her and urged her into a chair.

"Sally, what is it?" Guinevere demanded. "What's happened?"

Sally burst into tears and handed Guinevere a sheet of crumpled paper.

"Well, hell," Guinevere said as she read the message. "Looks like Zoltana is back in action."

The message was simple and to the point:

> THE PRICE FOR KEEPING YOUR PAST FROM HAUNTING YOU HAS JUST GONE UP. IF YOU WANT MY CONTINUED PROTECTION YOU MUST LEAVE ONE THOUSAND DOLLARS IN CASH AT A PLACE WHICH WILL BE MADE KNOWN TO YOU IN THE NEAR FUTURE. DO NOT HESITATE WHEN YOU GET MY NEXT MESSAGE. ALREADY I HEAR THE CHILD CRYING.

Guinevere's mouth tightened at the sheer cruelty of the words. With unsteady hands she refolded the piece of paper. "Did Ruth get one of these, too?"

"I don't know." Sally sniffed. "I haven't talked to her. I haven't talked to anyone but you."

Guinevere sat down beside her and took her hand. "Sally, you know what this is, don't you? It's blackmail."

"But Miss Jones, she was going to protect me."

"She has no power to protect you from the past. Only you can do that, by handling that past in a mature, adult fashion. Zoltana can't do anything except take your money."

"Oh, Miss Jones, I don't have a thousand dollars.

I'll have to get a loan, and who would loan me money to pay Madame Zoltana?"

"Even if you did come up with the cash, you couldn't give it to a blackmailer. You know that, don't you, Sally? You must understand that it wouldn't stop with the first thousand. It would just keep going on forever."

Sally drew a deep breath. "I knew when I got that note that I had to do something, Miss Jones. At first I was just paying for her psychic services. But it's gone beyond that now. I'm frightened."

"That's the only hold she has on you, Sally. As long as she thinks she can frighten you, she'll assume she can manipulate you. I'll bet she's not sending these notes to people like Mary and me, people who don't believe in her powers."

"It's different for you, Miss Jones," Sally said sounding defeated. "You're strong."

"So are you, Sally. Not many young women could have pulled themselves together the way you have after all you went through. You're one of the strong ones too. All you have to do is believe in yourself."

Sally looked up at her with a faint glimmer of hope. "Do you really think so, Miss Jones?"

"I really think so, Sally."

There was a short pause while Sally turned that over in her mind. "But what do I do now?"

"You will ignore this message, for one thing. For another, you and I are going to get some professional assistance in this matter. Madame Zoltana has gone too far this time. We amateur sleuths are going to call in the big guns."

"Guns?" Sally looked alarmed.

"A figure of speech," Guinevere assured her. She looked up at Trina. "Get Zac on the phone for me."

Sally looked startled. "Oh, please, I don't want anyone else to know about this!"

"Don't worry, Sally," Trina said gently. "Mr. Justis is very discreet. It's his business to be discreet. He's a confidential security consultant. He helps people who are being taken advantage of the way you are."

Sally didn't look convinced, but she waited in tense silence while Trina dialed Zac's number. Guinevere took the phone as soon as Zac came on the line. Quickly she spelled out what had happened to Sally.

"Tell her to call the Better Business Bureau and the cops," Zac said bluntly.

Guinevere smiled at Sally. "He says he'll help."

"Gwen!" Zac's protest came through the line with enough force to hurt her ear. "I did *not* say that. Don't you dare drag me into this. I've got enough on my hands as it is."

Confident that Sally couldn't overhear, Guinevere kept her smile firmly in place as she talked to Zac in soothing tones. "That's wonderful, Zac. Now, I figure the first thing we have to do is take a look around the premises."

"What premises?"

"Madame Zoltana's."

"Are you nuts?"

"I'll be glad to go by myself if you'd rather not accompany me," she said aloofly.

"Guinevere Jones," he began menacingly, "one of these days I swear, I'm going to . . ."

"Going to what?"

76

"We will discuss this after work," he informed her, and hung up in her ear.

Guinevere replaced the receiver and kept smiling confidently at Sally Evenson. "Don't worry," she announced. "Zac's going to help us. He'll handle everything."

Chapter Five

"I can't believe I let myself get talked into this." Zac glanced over his shoulder once again to make sure the night-dark back yard of Madame Zoltana's house was still empty. "I must be getting soft in the head. This is what comes of indulging women. They get uppity, demanding, and headstrong."

"I don't understand why you're complaining so much," Guinevere muttered as Zac used a thin strip of metal to work the back door lock. "You do this sort of thing all the time in your line of work."

"Rarely do I do this kind of thing in my line of work," he retorted. "I find that lately I'm doing it chiefly when I'm mixed up in one of your grand schemes."

The lock surrendered in his hands and the back door swung open with a faint squeak. Zac stood on the threshold, listening.

"What do you think?" Guinevere asked softly.

"I think no one's home."

"Well, we already know that. We knocked on the front door first, remember? And tried the phone. What can you see?" She prodded him forward until they both stood in the silent kitchen. Zac closed the door behind them.

"Did she have any pets?" he asked.

Guinevere shook her head. "None that I saw. Sally hasn't mentioned any either." She wrinkled her nose. "But she does smoke, as you may have noticed." The stale smoke smell hung in the air, probably absorbed in the drapes and imbedded in the furniture. "I think this place has been closed for several days."

"I think you're right. But then, you already knew that, didn't you?" Zac moved slowly through the kitchen. "Remember what I told you. Don't touch anything."

"I heard you." Guinevere peered around his shoulder into the dark living room, an undeniable sense of excitement running through her veins. She ought to be ashamed of the emotion, but she couldn't pretend it didn't exist. "I can't see a thing. She left all the drapes pulled."

Zac removed a small pencil-size flashlight from the inside of his jacket. "Luckily one of us came prepared."

"I expected no less from you," she retorted with mocking admiration. "Now, where do we start?"

"Beats me. I'm a stranger here myself."

The withering look she shot him was lost in the shadows. "I wish you would take this more seriously. Come on, let's go down the hall to her contemplation room. That's where she holds her psychic sessions."

Zac shrugged and followed obediently. The contemplation room looked very much as Guinevere had last seen it. The crystal bowl was still sitting in the middle of the table.

"When she did her psychic bit in the dark room, I was almost sure the bowl glowed just a little. It was weird." Guinevere looked down into the crystal object. "I wonder how she did it."

"It's an old trick," Zac said. "There's a small drawer hidden under the table. Probably got a light bulb in it. The crystal bowl sits over a cutout on the table surface. The light shines up through it and into the bowl. Small-time stuff. Fell for it, huh?"

Guinevere sensed his grin. "I did not fall for it," she announced loftily. "I knew it was a trick. I merely wondered how it was done." She turned away from the table and walked around the room. "I wonder if she keeps any files on her clients?"

"I wouldn't be surprised. From what you've told me, she sounds like a real businesswoman." Zac played the light around the room. "But I don't see anything in here."

"Let's check the rest of the place."

They walked through the remainder of the small house. All the drapes were pulled and there was an ashtray in every room, the ashes and butts several days old. Zoltana's interesting collection of caftans was hung neatly in the bedroom closet. The dresser was full of clothing. There was no evidence of any filing cabinet, and the desk they discovered in the bedroom contained nothing helpful. A manual typewriter sat on top of it.

"There must be something, Zac," Guinevere said at the end of the short search.

"You mean, you hate to admit you just broke into someone else's house for no reason." He was using the flashlight to examine the inside of a closet.

Guinevere ignored that. "You said yourself she's a businesswoman. She must keep some kind of records.

What about a safe?" She led the way back to the living room.

"A safe?"

"In the wall, or something. You know, behind a picture." Impatiently Guinevere went to shift the large, ornately framed painting that hung on the wall behind the sofa. She jumped as Zac snapped at her.

"I told you not to touch anything."

"Okay, okay." She pulled her fingers away before they touched the frame. "Sheesh, what a grouch. But let's look, Zac. There could be something behind that picture."

He came forward, gingerly using a handkerchief to slide the painting out of the way, and shone the flashlight against the wall. There was no sign of a hidden safe. Thoughtfully, Zac let the painting slip back into place. "Maybe the floor," he said musingly.

"What about the floor?"

"A lot of people have small home safes installed in the floor. It would be easy enough to do in an old house like this, with wooden floors. Let's have a look."

Guinevere smiled to herself. "I'm glad to see you're finally taking a real interest in this project. Where do we start?"

"By lifting the rugs." He went down on one knee and eased up the corner of the large, flower-printed area rug on the floor in front of the sofa.

Guinevere got down beside him and together they rolled up the heavy rug. When they were finished Zac shone the flashlight over every square foot of the wooden surface, looking for a suspicious break in the lines of the boards. Nothing.

"How about the kitchen?" Guinevere suggested.

"I don't think so. The kitchen floor's covered with linoleum. You don't go rolling linoleum up every time you want to put something into your household safe." Zac got to his feet and started toward the hall. "Let's try in here."

There were two small rugs in the hallway. When they were rolled aside nothing was revealed except a discarded cigarette butt that had apparently fallen from one of the ashtrays. Guinevere let the last rug slide back onto the floor and sighed.

"This is depressing," she complained.

"Your problem is that you have a short attention span. Let's give the contemplation room a try." Zac led the way into the small room. "We'll have to move the table and chairs. Now, for Pete's sake be careful, and use that handkerchief I gave you."

"Sometimes you're extremely bossy, Zac."

"Women love masterful men."

She arched her eyebrows as she and Zac lifted the surprisingly heavy table aside. "Where did you hear that?"

"I forget. Ready? Let's have a look."

At first Guinevere saw nothing unusual when the carpet was heaved aside, but Zac went down on one knee almost at once, eyeing the line between two boards. "Here we go," he said softly.

Guinevere's sense of excitement grew at the soft note of triumph in his words. Zac's voice often got that way when he was on to something. "What is it?" She crouched down beside him.

"If someone were going to install a floorboard safe, this is the way it would look."

"I don't see anything."

"Watch." Zac pressed heavily on one of the boards. It gave almost at once with only a faint squeak of protest. Then something snapped as hidden hinges responded. A two foot square of floor popped up, revealing a dark hole. Zac aimed the flashlight inside. Metal gleamed. A numbered dial was visible.

"Zac! It's here. A real safe!" Guinevere was awed by the wonder of it all. "If she kept any useful records, I'll bet this is where they'd be. Makes sense she'd keep them here in her contemplation room."

"Mmm." Zac flashed the light around the interior of the opening. There was another discarded cigarette butt sitting near the safe, but other than that, nothing. Zac reached down and picked up the cigarette end, rotating it between his fingers.

"Put that down, Zac. It's dirty."

He gave her an odd look and obediently dropped the butt back into the dark space under the floor. "You know, you can be awfully bossy yourself at times."

"Men love masterful women. Okay, Zac," Guinevere announced cheerfully, "this is where you get to really impress me. I can't wait to watch you crack a safe."

He shot her a long-suffering glance. "I hate to disillusion you, but I am not much of a safecracker. Picking a few standard door locks is not in the same league as opening a safe, even a small one like this."

Her eyes widened in horror. "You mean you don't know how to open this thing?" In the dim reflection of the flashlight, she thought she saw his mouth curve faintly. "Zac?"

"Fortunately for my image, I don't have to try."

"What are you talking about?"

Zac leaned down and reached into the hole in the floorboards. He caught hold of the metal door of the safe and flipped it open. "Somebody else has already done the hard part for me."

Shocked, Guinevere stared down into the open safe. "Zac, it's empty!"

"Well, what did you expect? That she'd hightail it without first cleaning out any incriminating records?" Zac got to his feet again and let the hinged section of floor drop back into place. "Come on, there's one more thing I want to check. Did you bring that note Sally received?"

"You told me to bring it, remember?" Guinevere pointed out self-righteously as she dug the note out of her purse.

"And an extra sheet of typing paper?"

"Got it." She followed him down the hall again to the desk in Zoltana's bedroom. When Zac held out his hand she gave him the blank piece of paper and watched with interest as he inserted it into the type-writer. "Do you think we'll actually be able to tell if Sally's note was done on this typewriter?"

"Maybe. Maybe not. Sometimes these old portables are eccentric enough that it's easy to tell if a letter was typed on a particular machine. Here, you type. I'm not that good at it."

"I think I detect a little sex discrimination here." Guinevere stood in front of the machine and quickly duplicated Sally's note on the fresh sheet of paper.

"Good. Now wipe the keys and the knob. We'll take a look at the two notes when we get back to your place." Zac moved around the room as Guinevere carefully wiped away any fingerprints she might have left.

Aware of a new level of tension in him she finished the task and asked, "What's wrong, Zac?"

"It's time we got out of here. Come on, let's get going."

Guinevere didn't argue. She trusted Zac's instincts. If he was getting restless, it was time to go, even if he couldn't give her a specific reason. Without a word she followed him down the hall and out the kitchen door. A few minutes later they were climbing into his three-year-old Buick, which was parked in the next block.

Guinevere stared thoughtfully out the window as Zac started the engine and drove back down First Hill toward Pioneer Square. It was shortly after midnight. "I wish I knew what Madame Zoltana used to keep in that safe."

"Well, one thing is for certain; it doesn't look as if she's planning to be away a long time. Clothing still in the closet, food in the refrigerator. Wherever she went, she intends to come back soon. We're probably lucky she didn't walk in on us," Zac noted gloomily.

"The really interesting thing is that Francine Bates has also disappeared," Guinevere remarked. "I wonder if they took off together."

"You said Francine was still at Gage and Watson the day after you saw Zoltana?"

"Yes. And she was still there that afternoon when I couldn't get hold of Zoltana. But she seemed nervous, Zac. She definitely was not her usual self. Damn. I wish I'd had a chance to set my little trap, so I'd know for certain if she was the one working with Zoltana."

Guinevere brightened. "But it must have been her, Zac. She's definitely the most likely candidate."

"No one knows much about Zoltana," Zac said slowly, "but people know a few things about Francine Bates. It might be possible to find her."

"Ah-ha! And if we find her, we might be able to find out where Zoltana is. Good idea, Zac. Let's do that." Guinevere turned in the seat to gaze at him expectantly.

"You have a wonderful way of making everything sound simple, Gwen," Zac told her with a deep sigh.

"Zac, finding people is supposed to be one of your specialties."

"I suppose we might start with the sister," Zac said without much enthusiasm.

"The sister? Oh, that's right. Francine mentioned something about having a sister over on the coast." She frowned. "But Gage and Watson's personnel department isn't likely to help me find her, Zac. Personnel departments have policies about giving out that kind of information."

"I'll try it from my end. You see if any of the people she worked with knows anything about her sister."

Twenty minutes later in her apartment they put the two typewritten notes side by side on a table and examined them.

"Piece of cake," Guinevere gloated. "Look at the smudges on the *E* and *T,* and the way the lines aren't quite even. It doesn't take an expert to figure out these are both from the same machine."

"It also doesn't help us very much. It just means that she returned to her house at some point to type the note she sent to Sally."

"Don't be so gloomy, Zac. You have to look on the positive side. We're getting all sorts of information tonight. With this amount of data, I expect you to solve the case in no time."

"This is your case, remember? You're supposed to solve it."

Guinevere smiled sweetly. "I'm a businesswoman. I'm smart enough to hire a professional consultant when I need one."

His own smile was wicked as he dropped the notes onto the table and pulled her into his arms. "This high-powered consultant of yours is getting anxious about his fee. He wants a little on account."

"On account of what?" she teased, twining her arms around his neck.

"On account of it's after midnight, he's tired, and he needs a little loving-kindness." Zac bent his head to move his mouth lingeringly over hers. "Let's go to bed, Gwen."

She hesitated. "Maybe we should discuss the case some more, Zac. Shouldn't we make notes about everything we saw tonight at Madame Zoltana's, while it's all still fresh in our minds?"

"We've already spent half the night doing what you wanted to do. Now we're going to do what I want to do. Bed, Gwen."

"It's true, isn't it? You do have a one-track mind."

"Bed, Gwen." One arm draped around her shoulder, Zac guided her firmly down the short hall to the bedroom.

Guinevere cast one quick glance over her shoulder before they turned the corner. The two notes rested side by side on the living room table. When Zac flicked the light switch they were hidden in darkness. They were clues, Guinevere thought, a little worried. Maybe she ought to lock them up before going to bed. But before she could voice her concern, Zac was unbuttoning her shirt and sliding his hands inside the wasteband of her jeans. She sighed contentedly and leaned against him, delighting as usual in his solid strength.

A few minutes later when that strength enveloped her completely, she forgot all about the two notes lying side by side on the table.

Guinevere phoned Sally Evanson first thing the next morning. Sally had bravely gone in to work although, Guinevere knew, the note from Madame Zoltana must be preying on her mind. Aware of the younger woman's fragile hold on her self-control, Guinevere decided on a firm, upbeat, everything's-under-control approach.

"Sally? This is Guinevere Jones. I just wanted to tell you, Mr. Justis has made terrific progress in your case. He tells me he's very near to settling matters for you."

"Miss Jones, is that for real? What's he going to do?"

"He's going to make quite certain Madame Zoltana gets out of the blackmail business once and for all. You're not to worry about a thing. You could help him get things under control even more quickly, however, if you could remember anything Francine Bates might have told you about her sister on the coast."

"Francine!" Sally was shocked. "What's she got to do with this?"

"We don't know, Sally, but there is a possibility she might be able to tell us something useful. Mr. Justis wants to talk to her. No one knows where Francine is, but he thinks there's a chance she might have gone to stay with her sister. She's never mentioned any other relative, has she?"

"Not to me. I don't know, Miss Jones," Sally said worriedly. "I don't remember much about Francine's sister. She only mentioned her a couple of times. I think she said she spent Christmas with her last year." There was a long pause while Sally tried to remember what she could about the sister. When she spoke again her voice was hesitant. "It seems to me her sister's name was Dorothy or Donna, or something like that. I just can't remember."

"Do you think anyone else at work might? You could ask Ruth or Mary or one of the others. Perhaps Miss Malcolm would know."

"I'll try, Miss Jones. I'll call you back as soon as I talk to them."

"Thanks, Sally. I'll be waiting." Guinevere hung up the phone and tried to occupy herself with the usual morning chaos. But Trina was handling the flurry of panicked calls from employers who had just had essential personnel phone in sick. Guinevere spent most of the time making notes of everything she had seen in Madame Zoltana's house the previous evening. Zac was right about one thing. The unfortunate fact of the matter was that they hadn't learned all that much.

Sally finally phoned back half an hour later. "Hi, Miss Jones. I talked to everyone I could think of, and finally Ruth said she was sure Francine's sister's name was Denise. Denise Bates. She thinks she lives somewhere near Pacific Beach. That's all I could find out. I'm sorry."

"Sally, that's wonderful. You've been a tremendous help. I'll call you as soon as Free Enterprise Security finds out anything useful. And don't worry, Sally. Mr. Justis really does have it all under control."

"That's very reassuring, Miss Jones," Sally said with humble gratitude. "Thanks."

Three minutes later Guinevere was on the phone to Zac, who yawned in her ear when she gave him the news.

"Excuse me," he said politely. "I'm still working on my second cup of coffee. I think I'm getting too old for the late nights and wild life you lead, Gwen. You're going to have to slow down for me."

Guinevere said something short and rude. "We would have gotten to bed quite a bit earlier if you hadn't decided to take advantage of me. Now, quit complaining and tell me what you're going to do next."

"Have a third cup of coffee."

"Zac!"

"Okay, okay. A name and an approximate location should be sufficient. A little time on the telephone should give me an address for Denise Bates. I'll let you know when I've got it. Oh, by the way, I'm going to be a little late getting home tonight. I've got to see a new client around four thirty. Chances are I'll be tied up until six or so. Your turn to cook dinner."

The phone clicked in Guinevere's ear and she sat looking at the humming instrument. *I'll be home a little late tonight.* It was getting to be so casual, so understood, so very routine. Zac was practically living with her these days. Guinevere tried to decide just how she felt about that, but before she could come to any earthshaking decisions, Trina was interrupting to tell her about the latest crisis. Guinevere sighed and gave up the task of analyzing her relationship with Zac. There didn't seem to be much point analyzing it, anyway. It was just happening.

At five thirty that evening the doorbell chimed demandingly. Guinevere put down the knife she had been using to chop mushrooms and wiped her hands on a towel. It couldn't be Zac, unless he had lost his key. She went into the entry hall and peered through the peephole. A shaft of nervous unease went through her when she saw who stood on her threshold.

Frowning, Guinevere held the door open a few inches but did not stand aside invitingly. "Rick! What on earth are you doing here?"

He lounged in the doorway, golden eyes moving over her with a familiarity that did nothing to stem the anxiety Guinevere was feeling. She refused to let him see how he was affecting her.

"I came to see you."

"I'm busy."

He looked amused. "So I see. Cooking dinner for that big, plodding hulk you're dating these days? What a waste of time. You can do better than him, Gwen."

"I doubt it. Now, would you kindly leave? I've got a lot to do." Guinevere tried to shove the door closed but found it stopped by Rick Overstreet's shoe. She glanced down, annoyed, and the next instant he had pushed his way inside and was closing the door behind him. Guinevere glared at him, refusing to give in to the small, niggling panic that had sprung up out of nowhere. "I'm asking you to leave, Rick." She kept her voice steady and very, very cool.

"I'm not ready to leave." He prowled through her living room as though he found it fascinating. "I'm curious about you, Gwen. I want to see just how much you've changed. You were living up on Capitol Hill when I knew you. This is all new."

"How did you get my address?" she demanded icily.

"It took some work, but I managed." He scanned the books in her huge yellow bookcase, his hands shoved casually into the pockets of his slacks.

"Rick, I—"

He swung around abruptly, facing her. "I've been thinking about us, Gwen."

"I wish you wouldn't," she said bluntly, not liking the glitter in those golden eyes.

"I've decided there's unfinished business between us."

"No, Rick. You finished it before it even began. You must have known I'd never play the role of the other woman. Not for any man."

"I knew. That's why I never told you about Elena. But I wanted you, Gwen. After you lost your nerve and broke off what was between us, I told myself I'd give you some time to calm down. Then . . . things happened. I got the new position with Gage and Watson, and shortly after that Elena died. By the time everything had settled down I'd lost track of you."

"Not only lost track, but lost interest, too, I suspect. I'm sure you went on to bigger and better things—and more cooperative women. Don't try to pretend that what you felt was a timeless passion, Rick. You know as well as I do that you were only looking for a convenient affair. I realized that as soon as I found out you'd lied to me."

He shrugged. "It doesn't matter now. We've run into each other again. There was always something about you, Gwen. . . ." He let the sentence trail off, his eyes intent. "I've discovered I want you again."

Guinevere smiled wryly. "Only because you can't have me. I'm a challenge for you now because I didn't fall right back into your hands the moment you encountered me again. Forget it."

There was a flare from the gold lighter as Rick lit one of his elegant cigarettes. He exhaled deeply, fixing her with a lambent gaze through the smoke. "No," he said finally. "I don't think I will forget it. It's fate, Gwen."

"The hell it is." She held the door open for him. "Please leave," she said very steadily. "Now."

"Before the hulk gets here, you mean?"

"Before I lose my temper and call the police to throw you out!" Guinevere heard the edge in her voice and frantically tried to bring herself back under control. She must not let him affect her this way. She refused to let him frighten her. "Listen to me, Rick. I will try to spell this out as simply as possible. I am not interested in you anymore. I want nothing to do with you. Find some other woman to hypnotize, because I'm immune to your brand of charm. It's shallow and it's meaningless. *Now get out!*"

He approached her with indolent grace, eyes narrowed and gleaming. "You say I'm only attracted by the challenge? Better watch out, Gwen. You're making yourself more of a challenge each minute. Two years ago you got away with walking out on me, only because I had other things to handle at the time. But now it's different. Now I can do what I should have done then. Are you sleeping with the hulk or keeping him dangling, the way you kept me dangling?"

"That's none of your damn business."

He nodded as if she had answered his question. "You're sleeping with him, I'm sure of it. There's something about the way he looks at you, the way he touches you. He tried to warn me off the other day when he saw me with you, did you know that? In a way, that added to the challenge too. It would be interesting to take you away from him, just to see how he would react. All things considered, I'm afraid you're becoming damn near irresistible, Guinevere Jones. I want you, and this time I'm going to have you." He smiled grimly around the cigarette. "But first I think I'll let *you* dangle a bit. It will serve you right. It's time you learned a lesson."

"Rick, if you don't leave, I swear, I'll have you thrown out." Guinevere's teeth were locked together with tension. She watched him take the cigarette from his mouth and casually grind it out in a small pottery bowl that stood on the hall table. It was the bowl where Guinevere kept her car keys. She wanted to scream at him that he had no business using the lovely bowl for an ashtray, but common sense told her to hold her tongue. She wanted to do nothing that would give him an excuse for staying any longer, and losing her temper would accomplish only that. He would delight in making her lose control.

"Good-bye, Gwen." He nodded with a mocking courtesy and walked out the door.

Guinevere shut the door behind him and locked it,

leaning against it with her eyes closed in relief. Holding her breath, she waited for the sound of his footsteps to die on the stairs. Only after she heard the faint noise of the outer door closing did she release her breath. Her heart was pounding with a fear that seemed wholly out of proportion to the incident.

The first thing that caught her attention was the smell of cigarette smoke. Guinevere wrinkled her nose in disgust. It wasn't just that it was smoke, it was Rick Overstreet's smoke. She hurried around the room, opening the windows as wide as possible. She didn't want the smell in the apartment when Zac arrived. She didn't want to have to try to explain Rick Overstreet to Zac. Her own foolishness two years ago was a source of embarrassment, and Zac would simply not understand why the man felt he could show up at her apartment uninvited. Lately Guinevere had begun to sense the streak of possessiveness that ran through Zac. She didn't approve of it, but she had no wish to bring it to the surface. Far better to let sleeping dogs lie.

When she'd finished with the windows she grabbed the bowl from the hall table and took it into the kitchen. There she held the butt under running water until she was certain it was extinguished and tossed it into the trash can under the sink. She rinsed out the bowl and replaced it just as she heard Zac's key in the lock. Taking a deep breath, she managed what she hoped was a bright smile as he came through the door.

"You're late," she announced, going forward to kiss him with more passion than she'd intended.

"I've got an excuse. I think I've located Francine Bates's sister," he said.

Chapter Six

"She's over on the coast, all right," Zac explained as he lounged at the kitchen table while Guinevere finished preparing dinner. He rested one foot on the chair opposite the one he occupied and wrapped his large fist around the small glass of tequila. His tie had been discarded and his collar loosened. He was the picture of domesticity—relaxing after a hard day's work while watching the little woman bustle around the kitchen. Zac intended to take advantage of the domestic scene as long as Guinevere would allow him to do so. "I got an address and a phone number. I tried phoning, but there was no answer, so I'll try again tomorrow."

"What if we can't reach her?" Guinevere dumped the pile of mushrooms into a frying pan and let them sizzle in butter.

"I guess if we can't get hold of her in a couple of days we could drive over to the coast and see if we can find her," Zac said reluctantly.

"Good idea! I'm impressed that you found her so quickly." Guinevere picked up her wineglass and took a rather large swallow. "You really are awfully good at your work, aren't you, Zac?"

Zac blinked lazily, watching her movements with a shuttered curiosity. The tension in her this evening was new. He'd seen it the moment he'd come through the door. Because of it, he'd refrained from asking her who had been smoking a cigarette in the apartment before he'd arrived. He'd caught the lingering scent of burning tobacco as soon as he'd entered the hall. But before he could casually ask who'd been visiting, Guinevere had thrown herself into his arms. Instinct had warned Zac to wait and see. "In my own slow, humble way I try to do my job," he said with grave modesty. To his surprise she reacted strongly to the joke.

"You are not slow or humble or plodding or anything like it," Guinevere said fiercely. "You are downright brilliant at times."

"Gosh, lady, I didn't know I'd made such a great impression."

She turned back to the stove brusquely. "Well, you have. Are you ready? The salmon is done and so are the mushrooms."

Zac cocked one thick brow. "Salmon? Now I'm the one impressed. What did I do to deserve salmon tonight?" He swung his foot down off the chair and got up to pour another glass of tequila.

"Nothing special. I stopped by the market on the way home from work and spotted a great buy on salmon, so I got some for us. Ready?"

"I'm ready."

She continued to chatter throughout dinner. Zac let her, content to eat the beautifully poached salmon and listen to Guinevere's conversation. The truth was, most of the time he liked listening to her talk. She had a talent for soothing him or teasing him or nagging him or arguing with him that was very satisfying. Zac

97

had a feeling he could listen to her for the rest of his life, merely taking steps to close her mouth when he was ready to take her to bed. Maybe not even then. He liked the small, passionate sounds she made in bed. But there was no getting around the fact that her conversation tonight contained a thread of tension. Zac waited. He was a patient man and he'd always been good at waiting when it was necessary.

After dinner Guinevere sat back in her chair and drained the last of her wine. "That," she announced, "was terrific salmon, even if I do say so myself."

"It was," Zac agreed, smiling at her. "And this kitchen will smell of fish tomorrow if I don't empty your garbage for you tonight. I'll take care of it while you start the dishes."

"Why do I always get to start the dishes while you empty the trash? There's a male chauvinist pattern developing in this household, Zac Justis." But she got to her feet and began rinsing dishes under the faucet.

"Some things are biologically preordained," Zac explained as he hauled the garbage out from under the sink. "Women have evolved with a certain innate ability to do dishes and men seem to have gotten stuck with a talent for emptying garbage. I suppose it's all fair enough, when you consider the great cosmic scheme of things. Be back in a minute."

He opened a drawer and found a twist tie for the garbage sack, and headed for the front door. The building's garbage chute was located near the stairs in the outside hall. Standing before the metal panel that opened onto the chute, Zac caught the stale cigarette smell as he started to twist the tie around the plastic bag.

He stood still for a moment, thinking. Then he calmly opened the bag and glanced inside. He found the damp cigarette butt under the paper that had been used to wrap the salmon. Zac stared at it for a moment, and then twisted the bag closed and dumped it down the chute. He would be patient.

The damning photos arrived in Guinevere's mail the following day.

She had decided to go back to the apartment before returning to the office after lunch, and her mail had already arrived. The lack of a return address in the upper left-hand corner made her curious about the plain manila envelope. She tore it open with an inexplicable sense of urgency. The message was as straightforward as the one Sally Evenson had received. It also appeared to have been typed on the same typewriter. Madame Zoltana had been busy.

Guinevere stood in the hall of her apartment building, reading and rereading the message. IF YOU WOULD PREFER THAT MR. JUSTIS DID NOT SEE THESE PHOTOS YOU WILL STOP MAKING INQUIRIES ABOUT ME. I DO NOT APPRECIATE THE INTERFERENCE IN MY BUSINESS.

After having read the message through at least four times, Guinevere unwrapped the black-and-white photos with a sense of dread. She was not surprised when she saw the crude shots of herself lying naked in Rick Overstreet's arms. No, she was not surprised, but she was suddenly physically sick.

Stuffing the photos and the message back into the envelope, Guinevere ran up the two flights of stairs and stabbed her key into her lock. It took several tries before she could control her shaking hand long enough to get the door open. Her breath was coming in tight gasps and her stomach threatened to rebel. She was damp with perspiration. Blindly she groped her way down the hall to the bathroom and sat down on the edge of the tub, waiting to see if she was going to lose her lunch.

Crouched on the cold porcelain edge of the tub, she clutched the terrible envelope in both hands and thought, This was what it was like for poor Sally. I didn't understand. How could I have known how awful it really is. *Blackmail.*

The photos were fakes, of course. Someone had cleverly taken head shots of her and Rick and applied them to two anonymous nude bodies. But they looked perfectly real. Modern photography techniques could mask almost any kind of fakery.

She had never been to bed with Rick Overstreet, not two years ago, not this past week, not *ever.* But, oh God, the photos looked so real. What's more, they were definitely recent shots. She had not worn her hair that way two years ago. It was the way she wore it now. Zoltana had made certain these pictures appeared very current. Zac would have understood Guinevere's involvement in an affair with another man two years ago. He wouldn't appreciate having it thrown in his face—no man would—but he'd have understood.

But he would never tolerate being a cuckold. Zoltana had wanted her victim to see these shots, to know that if Zac saw them, he must certainly assume Guinevere was currently having an affair with Rick

Overstreet. Any man who looked at these photos would believe the worst.

Guinevere sat waiting for the nausea to pass and tried desperately to think. For a few perilous moments it all seemed too much. She wanted to run and hide from Zac and the world. The only way she could steady herself was by thinking of Sally Evenson. That poor, poor woman. How easy it had been to give her bracing advice and tell her not to worry. How easy it had been to hand out the usual trite words about never paying off a blackmailer. Only now, finding herself in the same position, did she know the sense of awful doom and the utter helplessness. Guinevere opened her eyes and stared across the room. At this moment she understood completely how any blackmail victim might commit murder. But she didn't even have that option. Madame Zoltana had disappeared.

The phone rang in the kitchen. For a moment Guinevere blocked the intrusion out of her mind. She couldn't handle anything as normal as the phone right now. Besides, she wasn't even supposed to be home at this hour of the day. But it rang again and again, and at last Guinevere responded out of the habit of a lifetime. Ringing phones had to be answered. Like a zombie she walked into the kitchen.

"Hello?"

"Gwen? What the hell are you doing home at this time of day?"

When she heard Zac's voice, Guinevere thought her throat would close up completely. "I had lunch nearby. Just thought I'd stop and grab my mail."

"I see. When I couldn't get hold of you at the office I decided to take a chance and try the apartment.

Trina said you should have been back from lunch by now."

"What did you want, Zac?"

"I was just doing my consultant's duty and reporting in. I still can't get hold of Denise Bates. I think we're going to have to drive over to the coast. What about tomorrow morning?"

She nodded, realized belatedly he couldn't see her response, and finally found her voice. "Yes. Tomorrow would be fine, Zac. I'll tell Trina she'll be in charge all day."

"Okay, then I'll make arrangements here. Maybe it's all for the best. I was supposed to meet with that crazy interior designer in the morning. This will give me a perfect excuse for canceling the meeting. Oh, by the way, the caterer called to discuss adding a basil dip, for the vegetables, and a bunch of miniature eggplants. I told him to forget both, but he insisted on talking to you first."

"I'll give him a call, Zac."

"I don't care what you do about the basil dip, but I do not want to waste a dime on eggplant, miniature or otherwise. I hate eggplant. Is that clear?"

"Yes, Zac."

"I mean it, Gwen. No eggplant," he said, suspicious of her quick, obedient response.

"I heard you. No eggplant. I'll call him this afternoon. Is that all, Zac?"

There was a short pause. "Are you going back to the office now?"

"Yes."

"I'll pick you up after work. We can walk back to your place together this evening."

102

Guinevere cleared her throat in a wave of panic. "Uh, Zac, you've been over here for dinner every night this week. And you've stayed the night every night this week. Don't you need to take care of some things around your own apartment? What about your laundry?"

"My laundry's under control, Gwen," he said laconically. "Don't worry, if you don't feel like cooking, I'll handle it. We can have tacos again."

She wanted to cry, and instead she had to sound calm and firm. "Zac, I think we need a little time apart, don't you? After all, we've been almost living together lately. I think . . . I think we're rushing things. We need to maintain our separate identities. We haven't really discussed this, I know, but I thought we understood each other. Please, Zac." She held her breath, knowing her inner agitation was showing and unable to control it.

There was another brief pause from Zac's end of the line, and then he said quietly, "I thought we understood each other too. I'll pick you up tomorrow for the drive to the coast. Have a good evening, Gwen."

When he gently hung up on her, Guinevere let go of the hold she had been maintaining while on the phone. The tears fell freely until there were no more left inside. Then she picked up the phone again, called the office, and calmly told Trina that she would not be in for the rest of the afternoon or tomorrow.

"Is anything wrong, Gwen?" Trina added, concern in her voice.

"No, Trina. Nothing's wrong." She replaced the receiver and went into the living room. There she spread out the awful photos on the coffee table and tried to imagine exactly how Zac would respond if he ever saw them. When her mind refused to form a picture of his reaction, she decided it was because she couldn't bear to think about it.

Feeling weary and drained, Guinevere leaned back against the couch cushions and wondered vaguely how Madame Zoltana had learned about her and Zac. She wondered how Zoltana knew enough to select Rick Overstreet to use in the photos. And she wondered how Zoltana had found out that Guinevere was making inquiries.

When she got nowhere with that line of questioning, she remembered something Zoltana had said about Zac. *You will not be able to trust him.*

"Oh, Zac," Guinevere whispered wretchedly, "it's not a question of trust." But it was, wasn't it? Yet how could any woman expect a man to look at such pictures and not believe the lie they portrayed? If only Rick Overstreet had not shown up in her life a second time.

Which led back to the interesting question of how Zoltana could have known about Overstreet. Someone at Gage and Watson might have seen them together, Guinevere speculated listlessly. Or perhaps Rick had commented on their past relationship. Gossip could have filtered back to Zoltana's informant.

Guinevere tried pursuing that line of thought for a while, but it led nowhere. Nothing led anywhere. All her thoughts were running in useless little circles. An hour later she was still sitting on the couch, staring helplessly at the photos.

Zac found his own apartment very dull and very confining. It was not a place of relaxation and refuge, and it hadn't been for some time, he realized. Guinevere's apartment was home now. And he hadn't been invited home this evening.

He sat with his feet propped on his coffee table and stared out of his high-rise window, watching night settle on Elliott Bay. He was on his second tequila and was seriously thinking of forgoing dinner altogether in favor of getting disgustingly drunk. He rarely got disgustingly drunk. He couldn't even remember the last time. Probably back in college shortly before he'd dropped out in his junior year. Maybe not even then.

He liked his tequila, but the truth was, he wasn't the type of man who did anything that would take him beyond his own self-control. Except make love to Guinevere Jones. Zac had to admit that when she came alive under his hands he forgot everything else in the world but their combined excitement and satisfaction.

He wondered what she was doing at this particular moment. Eating, probably. He glanced at his watch. No, by now she would have finished eating. It was almost seven thirty.

Why hadn't she wanted him there tonight? He had to face the fact that he might have worn out his welcome. Zac took another sip of tequila, and when he was tired of confronting that fact, he went on to the next fact, which was that Guinevere Jones had said she loved him. She belonged to him.

Maybe she just wanted some time to herself. Everyone needed time alone. She was right, he had practically moved in with her lately, and she wasn't accustomed to having a man in the house. Of course, the reverse was true too. He wasn't accustomed to living with a woman. They both had adjustments to make. They both needed time to make those adjustments. Perhaps he had been rushing things lately, but it had all seemed so right.

But tonight everything seemed very, very wrong. He didn't like the feeling. There was the same sense of wrongness he felt when a case was going sour. But this hardly constituted a Free Enterprise Security case. This was Guinevere Jones.

Zac's mind jumped to the matter of the cigarette butt in Guinevere's garbage. That led to the memory of her tension last night. She had even been tense in bed for a while. He hadn't tried to make love to her. Instead he had pulled her close, his arm wrapped around her bare waist, and just held her. Eventually she had fallen into a heavy sleep. When he knew for certain she was no longer awake, he, too, had been able to sleep.

The vague tension he had sensed in her last night was nothing compared to the tension that had gripped her this afternoon when he had phoned her at home. Hell, if it were any other woman, he would have thought he'd interrupted an afternoon tryst with a lover.

The tequila in his glass slopped onto the coffee table as that last thought flashed through his mind. No. Not Guinevere. She wouldn't do that to him.

The memory of cigarette smoke drifted through his mind again, nagging at him, refusing to let go.

She wouldn't betray him with another man. She

would be totally honest. She would tell him if she had fallen in love with someone else.

Unless she sensed how hard he would fight to keep her from walking out of his life.

She would still be honest. It was her nature.

This was getting him nowhere. He was a patient man, Zac told himself. A slow, patient, plodding man. Hell, the people he'd once worked with had called him the Glacier. But he had his limits. Zac set down the tequila glass and got to his feet. Taking his windbreaker out of the hall closet, he opened the door, went out into the hall, and took the elevator down to the lobby.

Out on First Avenue he caught a bus that took him to Pioneer Square. He got off near Guinevere's apartment house and stood on the sidewalk looking up at her window. The arched panes of glass were dark. If she wasn't home he'd go out of his mind.

He used the key she had given him to let himself inside the apartment house door, and then he steadily climbed the two flights to Guinevere's door. When he stood outside her apartment, he hesitated a moment, listening. Slowly he inserted his key into the lock.

Guinevere was stricken with a curious sense of inevitability when she heard the key turn in the lock. She didn't move, but she turned her head to look at him as he opened the door. She hadn't bothered to turn on the lights, and in the shadows he seemed to fill the doorway. Carefully she set down her half empty wineglass. She couldn't find any words, so she stared mutely. It was Zac who spoke first, not moving from the threshold.

"You want to tell me what this is all about?" he asked, far too softly.

"I can't."

"Why not?"

"Because I love you," she whispered hoarsely.

"Then you have to tell me," he said simply. He still didn't move. "I'll go crazy if you don't."

"You'll despise me if I do."

Unexpectedly he smiled at that. "You know that's not true."

She shook her head helplessly. "Please go away, Zac."

"Don't you trust me?"

She caught her breath. *You won't be able to trust him.* "She said I wouldn't, you know. That afternoon when I had the psychic session with Madame Zoltana, she said I would be afraid to trust you when the chips were down."

"And are you?" he asked heavily.

She considered the question for the thousandth time. "It isn't exactly a question of trust."

"Isn't it?"

Guinevere looked down at the envelope on the coffee table. "Yes," she said quietly, "I guess it is." She stood up, the sense of inevitability stronger than ever. There really was no alternative. Zac had to know, and she had to face his reaction, whatever it might be. She picked up the envelope and held it out to him. "I love you, Zac."

He closed the door and came forward to take the envelope from her hand. "I know," he said. Then he calmly reached out and switched on a lamp. He turned the envelope upside down, spilled the photos and the typed message out onto the table, and stood quietly looking down at them.

Guinevere looked down at the damning evidence, too, her emotions as chaotic as if she were seeing the photos for the first time. Her voice stark, she said, "They're fakes, Zac. I have never been to bed with Rick Overstreet. I swear I would never betray you with him."

"Don't you think I know that?" Zac asked with a curious half smile.

She looked at him, the emotional trauma of the past few hours plain in her eyes. "Oh, Zac!" Then he was holding out his arms and she was throwing herself against the safety of his chest, burying her face against his shoulder. She felt his arms tighten around her protectively, felt the strength in him, and then she was crying again. But this time the tears were the healing kind.

Zac held her for a long while, his hands moving on her back with strong, soothing movements that seemed to comfort him as much as they did Guinevere. He cradled her close until the tremors stopped shaking her body. Finally Guinevere lifted her head and looked up at him, her eyes still damp.

"I'm sorry, Zac. When I got home this afternoon and found those pictures, it was just more than I could handle. I couldn't think straight—couldn't think how to explain them to you. I was sure you would take one look at them and that would be the end of everything."

"That, sweetheart, is why blackmail often works. The victim is sure that if the secret is revealed, it will be the end of everything."

"But, Zac, there's no secret. It's all a fake. Photographic tricks."

"I know."

"But how can you be sure?" Guinevere wailed, irrationally upset by his calm acceptance of the horror that had nearly driven her out of her mind that afternoon. "You barely glanced at them. And even if you study them you can't tell where the photos of the heads were joined to the bodies. I know—I've been studying them for hours."

"Gwen, my love, you wouldn't do that to me. If you had fallen for someone else, you'd make a clean break with me first. You wouldn't betray me."

"I know, but . . ."

His mouth crooked faintly at the corners, and he reached down and scooped up one of the photos. "And even if I weren't such a trusting soul, I do have eyes, and a very vivid memory. I know every square inch of your sweet body, Guinevere Jones, and this ain't it. Whoever posed for the nude portion of this shot is a little too big on top and much too small on the bottom."

"What?" Guinevere tore her gaze from his face to look at the picture. In the photo, the man's hand was cupping the woman's breast, and there was no doubt that there was a fair amount of bosom left over. When Zac's hand covered Guinevere's breast, he cupped the whole of it in his fingers. Guinevere was not built like a centerfold model. She smiled mistily as she met Zac's eyes again. "Are you saying I'm flat-chested and plump in the rear?"

"I'm saying you're perfect the way you are," Zac said diplomatically, shoving the photos back into the envelope. "Do you mind if we put these away for now, and talk about them later? I've had a very difficult afternoon."

"Because of me?"

He nodded solemnly. "Because of you. Don't ever do that to me again, honey. I couldn't take it."

"Zac, I'm so sorry," she whispered. "I've been so scared."

"You should have told me immediately what had happened." He cradled her face between his palms, his eyes intent and serious. "You know that, don't you?"

"Yes. Now I do. But I was in shock most of the afternoon. I couldn't seem to think straight."

"And you're still used to handling your problems on your own, aren't you?"

"I suppose so. Not that I was doing much of a job handling this one. My God, Zac, now I know what poor Sally Evenson must have felt like when she got her note from Madame Zoltana. It's the most incredibly helpless sensation. You just want to reach out and kill the blackmailer."

Zac paused. "An interesting thought."

Guinevere tilted her head, not understanding. "What do you mean?"

"Just what I said. It's an interesting thought. But we will pursue it later, along with a few other outstanding questions."

"What questions?"

"Never mind. They can wait. Right now I can't. I am going to take you to bed, Guinevere Jones, and together we are going to reassure each other."

"Are we?" She smiled tremulously as his big hands slid over her shoulders and down to her waist.

111

"Can you think of anything else you'd rather do?"

"No." She wrapped her arms around him. "Love me, Zac. I've never felt as alone as I did this afternoon."

"Neither have I."

He picked her up and carried her into the bedroom, not bothering with the light. "Undress me, Gwen," he muttered as he began removing her clothing. "Undress me and tell me how much you want me."

"More than anything else in the world," she answered tightly as the melting heat flooded her body. She felt her shirt fall from her shoulders, and then he was cupping her small breasts, his fingers enclosing her completely. His palms moved tantalizingly on the nipples, coaxing them into tingling firmness.

Guinevere sighed and leaned against his chest as she pushed off his shirt. She threaded her fingers through the curling hair that tapered down to his flat, strong stomach. She could feel the hardness of him through the fabric of his slacks. His hands went around her, urging her close until the waiting heaviness of him was pressed against her soft thighs.

"I want you, Gwen."

"I know," she whispered as he tugged her jeans and panties down over her hips. Then he was lowering himself slowly to his knees, his mouth moving over her breasts and soft belly until her senses were reeling.

"Ah, *Zac.*" She inhaled sharply when he dipped his fingers between her legs and found the warm, silky moisture that betrayed her readiness. She steadied herself, her fingertips digging into his broad shoulders, as she felt his mouth in a stunningly intimate kiss. "Oh, my darling!"

112

"Come to bed, sweetheart. It's been a long day." He rose slowly, stepping out of his slacks. Gently he tumbled her down into the sheets and came down beside her, one thigh anchoring her firmly beneath him. "Wrap yourself around me and tell me I'm home."

"You're home, Zac. So am I."

Her fingers flicked along his hot skin, seeking the thrusting contours of his back and hips. When he pushed her thighs apart with one hand and settled himself between her legs she urged him closer with eager hands. She loved the heavy weight of him along her body, loved the full, waiting male power in him. Most of all, Guinevere realized, she loved Zac Justis.

He came to her with a sure, surging strength that filled her completely, unleashing the exciting, twisting rhythms of her own body. She moved beneath him, glorying in the almost savage force of his possession. Her nails bit into his back with feminine hunger. Guinevere gave herself completely when she gave herself to Zac, and he responded just as totally. Neither of them held back anything during these wild, sweet moments of physical union.

When the culmination overtook them, it did so almost simultaneously. Guinevere was unaware of how Zac made himself wait so that he could watch the passion in her face as she cried out his name, but she heard his echoing response a moment later and felt the shudders of his hard, solid body.

When it was all over, Guinevere turned and nestled against Zac's warm body, content at last and ready for sleep.

"Not just yet, Gwen," Zac said quietly. "You can sleep later. Right now we're going to talk."

Chapter Seven

"Who is Rick Overstreet?" Zac asked. "I'd like the whole story this time."

Guinevere stirred in the cradle of his arm. "Do we have to talk about him now?"

"Mmm. I think so, yes."

She sighed, knowing there was no way of postponing the discussion. When Zac asked a direct question in that tone of voice, he didn't let go until he had the answer. Guinevere knew better than to argue. "Rick Overstreet was a mistake."

"An old lover?" His voice was almost perfectly neutral.

"No. I told you, I've never been to bed with him. Not recently and not two years ago, when I met him. But I dated him for a while. I met him while working at the company he was with at the time. I was with a temp firm. It was shortly before I opened Camelot Services. Rick can be very . . ." She broke off, looking for the right word. "Very charming. He has a way of casting out lures to women. Two years ago, I suppose I had hopes that something more might develop between us."

"What happened?"

"I found out that he was married. He hadn't bothered to inform me of that fact. When I realized he'd lied to me and saw him for what he was, I told him I had no intention of being the other woman."

Zac considered that for a long moment. "Didn't he tell you he was on the verge of divorcing his wife? That's the usual line in a situation like that."

"It wouldn't have made any difference, because I'd never marry a man who divorced his wife because of me. But now that you mention it, no, he never did try that line. Maybe he realized it wouldn't have worked. I was very angry at the time, and I made it very clear I never wanted to see him again."

"He let you go without a fight?" Zac sounded skeptical.

Guinevere smiled, her lips moving slightly against his chest. "Not everyone is as tenacious as you are."

"I wouldn't have let you walk out that easily."

She lifted her head and looked down at him. "You wouldn't have lied to me about a wife in the first place."

"No," he agreed, watching her face. He was quiet for another long moment. "You ran into Overstreet again at Gage and Watson, didn't you?"

Guinevere nodded. "I suppose it was bound to happen sooner or later. Seattle isn't that big, and I have contacts with many of the companies with offices downtown. As long as he and I were both working in downtown Seattle, the possibility of running into him existed. Frankly, I hadn't worried about it, because I hadn't given him much thought in the past two years. He hadn't thought about me very often, either, as far as that goes. He admitted it. A lot of things happened to him shortly after I stopped seeing him. He got distracted, I suppose. And then, knowing him, there would have been other women closer at hand than I was."

"What kind of things distracted him?"

"Well, his wife died, for one thing. And he got a new job. The position at Gage and Watson, I guess. I don't know what else might have happened. I haven't talked to him that much. Just a few times in the hall at Gage and Watson."

"So he wrote you off until he ran into you again at Gage and Watson. Did he tell you right away that his wife had died?"

"Well, yes," Guinevere admitted.

"And then he decided to see if he could pick up where he left off two years ago."

"I told him I wasn't interested," Guinevere said earnestly, alarmed by the emotionless tone of Zac's voice. "It was the truth."

He looked at her through lazily lowered lids, which concealed the expression in the ghost-gray eyes. "But he's still trying?"

Guinevere took a deep breath. "I think he sees me as a challenge now. Unfinished business. He came over here last night, before you got here."

"I know."

Guinevere's eyes widened. Then she nodded slightly. "Yes, you do, don't you? I should have known."

"Why didn't you tell me?"

"Because I wasn't sure what you would do. I was afraid things might get violent if you knew he was pestering me. I didn't want you involved in a brawl on my behalf. I also felt that Rick Overstreet was my

116

problem, something I had to handle. I'm a big girl, Zac. I'm supposed to be able to handle my own problems. And I *am* dealing with him."

"The hell you are. He's hunting you. I saw his face the other day when you got off the elevator with him. And now he's come to your apartment."

"I threw him out!"

"Next time I'll throw him out," Zac told her evenly. "That should settle the matter."

"Zac, you make me sound like a stupid, silly little female who can't handle a man who's making a pass." Guinevere realized she was beginning to sound shrewish. "I'm thirty years old, and I am not weak or stupid or silly. Furthermore, I do not want any violence. Do you understand?"

"Let's forget that subject and go on to the next."

"Which is?" she asked, suspiciously, not ready to let go of the first topic of discussion.

"Those pictures in the envelope."

The fight went out of Guinevere. She collapsed against him. "My God, Zac, I thought I was going to be sick when I saw them. I never knew how bad blackmail really is. It hits you right in the stomach. When I think of all the little lectures I gave Sally, I get thoroughly disgusted with myself. I didn't really understand what she was going through."

"Don't knock your little lectures to Sally. From what you've told me, they helped her a great deal. She was actively helping us find Francine Bates's sister, wasn't she? She has the feeling that something is being done. She's fighting back. That's the important thing, Gwen."

"You're right. It's the feeling of being totally helpless that gets you. Like I said, I just wanted to commit murder."

"Yes. The thought has crossed my mind more than once this evening. Gwen, if it's crossed our minds, I'm sure the solution has occurred to a few other people too."

"What do you mean?"

Zac crooked an arm behind his head, his brows meshing into a thick line above his narrowed eyes. "Maybe Madame Zoltana is lying low because she's nervous about one of her 'clients' doing something drastic."

"You read that note she sent. She wants me to stop making inquiries."

"Which means," said Zac, "that she knows you've been making them. She also knows something about you and Rick Overstreet. At least, she knew enough to use him in her threat. She must have realized that photos of you with that particular man would really upset you, because you had a link to him in the past. You must be right about her having an insider at Gage and Watson."

"I suppose anyone could have seen me talking to Rick in the hall at work and then seen me with you. Whoever saw me could have put two and two together. It's even possible Rick made some comment. I wouldn't put it past him to . . . to imply things to other men. You know what I mean." Guinevere paused a moment. "I get a little nervous around Rick," she went on in a low voice. "I don't like him. Someone might have noticed that I wasn't comfortable with him and decided to use the information somehow. I still think the most likely candidate is Francine Bates."

"We'll see what we can find out in the morning." Zac's voice changed abruptly, returning to normal. Gently he lifted her aside and pushed back the sheet. "Hungry?" He slapped her lightly on her lush rear.

Guinevere blinked. "I hadn't thought about it."

"Well, I am. I didn't have dinner tonight. Too busy sitting alone in my apartment stewing over you. I'm going to fix myself a bite to eat. Taking you to bed always gives me an appetite."

Guinevere smiled, watching him as he walked across the room to retrieve his Jockey shorts. Then he disappeared into the bathroom. She liked the solid, hard planes of his body. There was something very substantial about Zac, both physically and mentally. She got to her feet and reached for a robe.

A few minutes later she found him in the kitchen, slicing cheese and arranging crackers on a plate. He was eating a saltine as he worked. She watched him from the doorway for a moment.

"Thank you, Zac," she said softly.

He looked up, still munching. His ghost-gray eyes were full of the rare warmth he reserved for her alone. "For what?" he asked around the cracker.

"Believing me."

He swallowed the cracker. "Next time something like this happens, keep in mind that you could tell me the IRS is a benevolent association devoted to the preservation of hamsters, and I'd believe you." He popped another cracker into his mouth.

Guinevere came up behind him and wrapped her arms around his waist. "I love you, Zac."

He turned around, smiling, and shoved a cracker into her mouth. "I love you, too. Let's eat."

After a fairly lengthy drive, Zac and Guinevere reached the coast around nine o'clock the next morning, and sometime later they finally found the Bates cottage. It took three stops to ask directions and several wrong turns, but at last Zac was parking the Buick on the side of the road in front of the weathered, gray structure. He sat for a moment with his hands on the wheel, studying the house.

The cottage was quite isolated. It sat alone on a bluff overlooking the ocean. There was a thick group of trees to the rear that marched up a hill and disappeared on the other side. A car was parked out front.

"I think the best way to handle this is the straightforward approach," he finally said. "I could pretend to be an insurance salesman or something, but I think that would be a waste of time."

"Do you think anyone's at home?" Guinevere peered at the cottage windows.

"I think so. Let's go." He got out of the car and walked around to the passenger side to open Guinevere's door.

The brisk breeze off the sea caught her neatly bound hair as she stepped out of the Buick, sending wispy little tendrils fluttering around her face. Guinevere automatically put up one hand to keep the hair out of her eyes as she followed Zac to the front door.

It took three knocks before anyone answered. The woman who reluctantly opened the door appeared to be in her late fifties or early sixties and resembled Francine Bates. She wore her blond tinted hair in a short, curling bob, and looked at Zac with suspicious eyes.

"Yes? What do you want?" she asked bluntly.

"We're here to see Francine Bates. Please tell her it's important and that we won't be leaving until we've talked to her."

"She's not here." The woman tried to close the door, but found its progress impeded by the presence of Zac's foot. "Now, look here, mister—"

"Justis is the name. Zachariah Justis. My friend here is Guinevere Jones. Francine knows her."

"I don't see what that has to do with anything. I've told you my sister isn't home!" The woman looked desperately at Guinevere, as if hoping she would find the woman less implacable than the man. "Please, I'm telling you she isn't here. I haven't seen her in ages. She lives in Seattle."

Guinevere sensed the near hysteria in her voice and moved closer, smiling gently. "It's all right, Miss Bates. I only want to talk to your sister. It's very, very important. We've been trying to find her for several days. Please help us."

"What's going on here?" the woman demanded shrilly. "I tell you, I've had it with all this nonsense. I can't take any more. Now, get out of here and don't come back, do you hear me?"

Guinevere sensed Zac was about to move forward aggressively. She put her hand on his arm and spoke again soothingly to the woman. "Please, Miss Bates. We must talk to her. A great deal depends on what she can tell us about Madame Zoltana."

The older woman opened her mouth to protest once more, but her words were cut off by another voice.

Francine Bates appeared behind her sister, her face drawn and tense. She looked at Guinevere, ignoring Zac.

"It's all right, Denise. I knew that sooner or later someone would find me," she said wearily. "Let them in. I'll talk to them."

There was a moment of silent tension as the four people regarded one another, and then Denise opened the door to admit Zac and Guinevere. She stood stiffly aside as they entered.

"Sit down," Francine said quietly. "Denise, would you fix us all some tea?"

Denise hesitated, her eyes on her sister. Then she turned and marched into the kitchen.

Guinevere glanced around at the comfortable old cottage, with its old-fashioned, slightly shabby furniture and the amateurish seascapes on the walls. She sank into the depths of the sofa and Zac sat down beside her. Francine sat across from them, still looking only at Guinevere.

"You've found me," Francine said finally. "What do you want?"

It was Zac who responded, hard, his voice dark. "Some answers."

Francine nodded to herself. "Yes, I guess you do. I wish I had all of them."

Guinevere leaned forward. "Francine, tell me. Were you Madame Zoltana's inside woman at Gage and Watson? Was it you who told her who I was and gave her the kind of information she needed to impress her clients?"

Francine's mouth tightened. Her hands clenched in

122

her lap. "It seemed harmless at first," she finally whispered. "Just a game. Everyone got a kick out of it."

"And Madame Zoltana split the twenty dollar fees with you?" Zac asked, hazarding a guess.

Francine flashed him a quick glance and nodded. "I realized it was getting to be more than a clever little game, but somehow I couldn't stop it. Zoltana seemed to have certain people hooked. She kept making them return, and the fees she charged got higher. But people like Sally and Ruth seemed to want to go back to her."

"How did you meet her?" Guinevere asked kindly.

Francine sighed. "By accident. I went to her myself one day for a psychic reading. I was just curious, you understand. I don't really believe in that stuff. But she was good. Very clever. I was intrigued. When it was over, she suggested I tell some of my friends at work. She said she would give me a finder's fee for every new client I sent to her. I didn't see anything wrong with that, so I agreed. I got a fee even if someone else made the appointment for a new client, the way Ruth did with you."

Zac shifted slightly on the old sofa. "But things got more complicated, right? The next thing you knew, she was asking you for information about the clients before she gave them their sessions."

Francine looked at him helplessly. "She just wanted to know a few details here and there. Said it would make the sessions more entertaining for the people." Francine bit her lip. "She also said she would give me a larger percentage of the fee. I shouldn't have done it. I know I shouldn't have done it. But somehow it was all so easy, and I needed the money, and I didn't think

I was really hurting anyone, and . . ." Her voice trailed off as she looked down at her twisting hands.

"Where is Madame Zoltana, Francine?" Zac asked.

"I don't know." The response was barely audible. She didn't look up.

"Yes, you do," Zac insisted.

"No! I swear I don't know." Francine's head lifted. Her eyes held a look of desperation.

"But you're afraid," Zac went on ruthlessly. "You disappeared a day or two after Zoltana did. Why?"

"Because I don't know what happened to her! Don't you understand? I'm afraid that whatever happened to her might happen to me. If anyone guessed that I worked with her . . ."

"What makes you think anything did happen to her?" Zac demanded.

Francine shook her head again. "I don't know. It's just a feeling. I went to her place that evening after Guinevere had her appointment, just like I always do, to collect my share of the week's fees. But she wasn't there. I tried her again later that night and she still wasn't there. I began to get worried. Zoltana never went out at night, you see. She was home most of the time, in fact. Every time I saw her, she was cooped up in that dark house with all the drapes pulled and the smoke so thick you could cut it with a knife. She told me once she couldn't stand being out at night because it made her nervous. I teased her about being afraid of ghosts or something, and she just looked at me and said it was the truth. I believed her. You see, I—I got to know her a little during the months I was sending clients to her. Once in a while, she talked to me when I went to get my cut. I think I'm probably the only one

124

she ever did talk to about anything personal. She was a very odd woman in a lot of ways. Sometimes I got the impression she really did think she had a few of those psychic powers she pretended to have."

The woman's fear was a tangible thing. Guinevere could feel it emanating from her in waves. "Francine, what is it? Do you think one of Zoltana's clients got angry enough to do something drastic? Who would do such a thing? I've seen the ones she really victimized. They were people such as Sally Evenson and Ruth what's-her-name at Gage and Watson. Zoltana knew what she was doing. She picked on the fragile people, the ones who wouldn't fight back. From what I can tell, Zoltana was a shrewd operator. She wouldn't have tried to run her scam on someone who might have retaliated."

Francine sucked in her breath and reached for a hanky just as Denise returned with the tea tray. Francine stared at the teapot, gathering her self control.

"I think she had something else going on besides the psychic sessions," Francine said after a long moment.

Zac pounced. "What makes you think that?"

"Something she said a couple of times. I once asked her if she was really making much of a living off the psychic sessions, and she told me it was enough to get by on but that she had a . . . a pension plan for her old age."

"A pension plan?" Guinevere stared at Francine's troubled face.

"She used to say that every time she looked into her bowl, she saw a comfortable future for herself. I couldn't figure out what she was talking about, so one night I asked her. She just said she had something big going on the side. Something that was making a lot more money for her than the piddling little psychic sessions, and that in another couple of years she was going to have enough to retire and move to Arizona."

"All right, Francine," Zac said flatly, "what do you think she had going on the side?"

Denise spoke up before her sister could respond. "Franny, no, don't say anything. I think you should keep quiet about this."

Francine gave her a bleak glance. "Why, Denise? If they found me, someone else could too. What good does keeping silent do? We can't stay locked up in this house forever."

Denise closed her eyes and sat back in her chair.

"Well?" Zac prompted with a ruthlessness that made Guinevere wince. The man had no subtlety, but he got answers.

"I think," Francine said slowly, "that Zoltana was blackmailing someone."

Guinevere frowned. "All her little scams could be called blackmail."

"No, not those little twenty- and thirty-dollar psychic sessions she conned people into. I mean real blackmail. Thousands of dollars. I think she had someone important on the hook and that person finally figured out who was doing it."

"And you think that same someone killed her? You think she's dead?" Zac concluded.

Francine nodded miserably. "I'm afraid that if he or she ever finds out I was working with Zoltana, I'll be next. Whoever it is will assume I know whatever it is that Zoltana knew."

"But you don't," Guinevere said.

"No. If I did, I'd know whom I had to fear, wouldn't I? As it is, I'm living in terror of almost everyone. It's very hard to live that way, Gwen. The truth is, I was almost glad to see you standing out there on the porch a few minutes ago. I knew you must have come about Zoltana, and I didn't think you could be the one she was blackmailing."

"Why not?"

Francine shrugged. "I don't know. I just didn't think the killer would look like you." She swung her weary gaze to Zac. "Him, maybe, but not you."

"Zac is investigating Madame Zoltana's disappearance," Guinevere said firmly. "He's not interested in killing her."

"Yet—at any rate," Zac added laconically. "Francine, what would you say if I told you we have some reason to think Zoltana is still alive?"

Francine looked startled. "You do?"

"Since she disappeared, two different people have received blackmail threats. Not penny-ante stuff, but real threats."

"I don't understand," Francine said in confusion. "I've been so convinced that she must have been killed, I can hardly believe she's alive."

"We don't know if she is or not. There's another possibility," Zac went on, ignoring Guinevere's questioning glance. "You might be right. Whomever she was blackmailing might have killed her and then decided to use her files to continue fleecing her victims. He or she might not have been able to resist the easy pickings. One thing's for certain, the price of Zoltana's

127

silence has risen considerably. One threat said the pay-off would be a thousand dollars."

"Good lord," Francine whispered. "I don't under-stand this. I just don't understand."

"Neither do we," Zac informed her, "but we're go-ing to find some answers. That's why we're here." He pulled a notepad out of his jacket pocket. "Let's run through everything again, Francine, step by step. I want you to try to remember every conversation you had with Zoltana concerning her 'pension plan'."

Denise shuddered and looked at her sister. "What's going to happen?"

"Whoever has decided to go into blackmail in a big way is going to find that it doesn't always pay," Zac said softly. "He or she has already made one serious mistake."

"What's that?" Francine asked urgently.

"Whoever it is tried to blackmail Gwen," Zac ex-plained calmly. "That's the end of the line." His ballpoint pen clicked. "Now, tell me again about Zoltana looking into her own future."

Guinevere sat back and watched Zac lead Francine Bates through a detailed history of her association with Madame Zoltana. It took almost an hour, and Zac had the blunt techniques of an inquisitor. At the end of the hour poor Francine Bates was exhausted. When Zac finally closed his little book with a snap the older woman looked at him anxiously.

"What should I do now?"

"Stay out of sight while I see what I can do back in Seattle. We know the envelopes containing the new blackmail threats were mailed in the city, so chances are whoever's behind them, whether it's Zoltana or someone else, is still in town. I'll be in touch as soon as I know anything."

"But, Mr. Justis, I'm frightened," Francine said as Zac got to his feet.

"Maybe you should have thought about that before you started helping Zoltana con people like Sally Evenson," he remarked, taking Guinevere's arm and heading toward the door. He didn't wait for a response. He pushed open the door, got Guinevere outside, and let the screen slam shut behind them.

"You were rather hard on her, Zac," Guinevere said quietly as they walked to the car.

"No, I wasn't. You've seen me when I come down hard on people, Gwen. I treated Francine Bates with kid gloves, and you know it."

Everything was relative, Guinevere decided as she slipped into the front seat of the Buick. She had seen Zac pin a man against a wall by the throat while he asked his questions. Compared to that, she supposed it could be said that Zac hadn't been hard on Francine Bates.

"Do you think she's safe here?"

"I don't know," Zac admitted as he put the car in gear. "But I can't protect her and she's not willing to go to the police, so there's not much anyone can do except try to find out what happened to Zoltana. That's the only way to put a stop to this mess."

"What do we do next?"

"Eat. It's almost noon."

"Be serious, Zac."

"I am serious. I've got a taste for razor clams, and this is supposed to be a good place to find them. Let's go find a restaurant."

There was something about his voice that alerted her. "You're on the edge of Deep Think," she accused.

"Deep Think?"

"You know, when you turn off the outside world and go someplace inside your head and think. You always do it when you're getting near the turning point in a case. Before you do, tell me what you think happened to Zoltana. Do you believe she might have been killed?"

"It's a possibility. If Francine's right about there being a major blackmail victim somewhere in the picture, someone who was shelling out thousands of dollars for Zoltana's silence, then, yes, it's a possibility."

"And that same someone might have discovered her client files and decided to try to get what he or she could out of them." Guinevere thought about it. "Whoever it was had to know I was starting to ask questions."

"True. Which suggests that if someone else is involved, he or she is probably associated with Gage and Watson."

"Or knows Sally Evenson. Sally might have said more than she should have, if someone pumped her carefully enough. She's very sweet, but not the most sophisticated thinker in the world."

"She was afraid of Madame Zoltana. Do you think she might have killed her, Gwen?"

"No."

"Are you sure? Anyone can kill, given the right set of circumstances," Zac said.

"You have a very low view of human nature."

"I have a realistic view of it."

Guinevere turned the matter over in her mind. "I

suppose Sally might have been capable of murder if she was sufficiently frightened. But I don't see her figuring out how to get rid of the body, or how to open the safe. Furthermore, I don't think she'd try to blackmail Zoltana's clients. It just isn't in her to be that organized and ruthless, Zac. Murder in the heat of fear and anger, possibly. But not cold-blooded blackmail later."

"Okay, who does that leave?"

Guinevere ran through the list of people who had gone to Madame Zoltana. "There's Ruth. But she's a lot like Sally. Then there's Mary, who's much tougher. One or two others. But Zac, why assume Zoltana's dead? Those last blackmail threats came from her typewriter, don't forget."

"I haven't forgotten. But if someone killed her, it would make sense for the killer to make it look as if Zoltana was still behind the blackmail attempts. It would be simple enough to slip back into Zoltana's house and use the typewriter."

The razor clams were perfectly fried and accompanied by huge, chunky fries. Guinevere and Zac ate their fill in a rustic little café down by the water's edge, and afterward drove back to Seattle.

Zac moved in and out of what Guinevere termed Deep Think during most of the long drive home. He would surface long enough to ask her a question or two and then grow silent again, driving without a word for long stretches of time. By the time they reached Seattle he had almost ceased communicating altogether. Guinevere waited patiently for the results, but none were forthcoming.

As soon as they reached Guinevere's apartment,

Zac checked in with his answering service. He hung up the phone with an expression of satisfaction on his face.

"Well, one good thing came out of today, at any rate. Gertie says Evelyn Pemberton tried to get in touch to tell me she's going to acccpt the job. She says we can discuss the pension plan next week. What a relief."

"I was sure of her all along," Guinevere informed him confidently.

"I'm glad somebody was. Now, as long as I don't find any eggplant being served at the party, I will count myself a reasonably lucky man."

Zac awoke early the next morning, fully alert and hating the uncomfortable sensation of being too *aware*. It meant matters were getting serious. He rose on one elbow and looked down at Guinevere, who slept peacefully curled against him. Whoever had tried to terrorize her would pay a heavy price. Attacking Guinevere was not within the rules of the game. Since Zac had made this particular rule himself, he intended to enforce it.

Chapter Eight

At eight o'clock on the morning after the interview with Francine Bates, Zac sat at his desk and gazed moodily out of his cubicle window. The view across the hall was as uninviting as ever. The salesman who usually occupied the cubicle on the other side of the corridor was out of town and had left his drapes pulled. Zac was staring at a wall of beige drapery, which did nothing to stimulate his mental acuity. He was looking forward to having a real view when he moved upstairs the following week.

Zac was steadily working his way through his second cup of coffee while he considered everything he had on the Madame Zoltana mess. The more he thought about it, the more he decided to spend the morning tying up a couple of loose ends. They might or might not relate directly to the matter, but in any event, his own curiosity would be satisfied. Zac finished the coffee and decided to walk down Fourth to the Seattle Public Library as soon as it opened.

Two hours later he was seated in front of a microfilm reader scanning the obituary sections of two-year-old editions of the Seattle *Times* and the *Post Intelligencer.* It took a while, but with the help of a librarian and an index he found what he wanted. Overstreet was not a very common name. The obituary on Elena Overstreet was brief and to the point. In a copy of one of the other papers he found a short article on Mrs. Overstreet's death. Zac dug out his notebook and made a few entries. Then he thanked the librarian and went back to his office to see how good his newly formed contacts with the police were. Shortly before lunch Zac called Guinevere.

"I'll pick you up in a few minutes. We have a few things to talk about."

Guinevere hung up the phone feeling uneasy. Zac's voice had taken on that cold, detached manner it always had when he was closing in for the kill.

The kill. It was only a casual phrase used to describe the finale of a case, but somehow the words seemed underlined in her mind. Guinevere shook off the feeling and turned to Trina.

"Mind if I take lunch first? Zac's on his way over. He wants to talk to me about the Zoltana case."

"No problem. I'm supposed to be dieting this week, anyway. Take your time, but think of me while you're wolfing down french fries and spinach pasta."

"French fries and spinach pasta?"

"That's what I'm craving at the moment."

When Zac arrived a few minutes later, it was clear that food was not uppermost in his mind. The night before Zac had been sliding in and out of his Deep Think state. Today she knew instinctively he was on the edge of that other state of being she had seen him in when a case was closing. He was turning into a hunter. It was on these occasions that Guinevere was painfully conscious of the essential core of hardness in the man.

134

"I'm supposed to order french fries and spinach pasta," she said lightly as they walked the two blocks to the waterfront.

"We'll eat at a fish and chips stand. I don't want to waste time at a full-service restaurant," Zac said flatly.

"Well, at least I'll get the french fries," Guinevere muttered to herself. This was not the time to argue. Zac had his mind on something else.

They gave their orders at the counter of a sidewalk fish bar and waited until the trays were ready. Then they carried the food to the patio eating area and sat down across from each other.

"Okay, what gives?" Guinevere couldn't stand the suspense any longer.

"I did a little checking this morning."

"On what? Or should I say, on whom?"

"On Rick Overstreet." Zac reached for the vinegar bottle.

Guinevere halted the french fry that was halfway to her mouth. "Why?" she asked simply.

"Curiosity. Plus the fact that he's at least peripherally involved in this case. Don't forget that whoever was trying to put pressure on you knew there was some reason you would panic at the sight of photos of you and Overstreet. That means someone knew the two of you were more than passing acquaintances."

"Not necessarily," Guinevere said slowly.

"Blackmail works on an emotional level. That means there has to be something emotional on which the blackmailer can base the threat. Somebody knew he or she could scare you to death with a threat involving Rick Overstreet. The next question we have to ask ourselves is whether Zoltana would know that much about you and Overstreet."

"If Rick had talked about us at work," Guinevere began uncertainly, not wanting to speculate on what he might have said, "someone could have heard and reported to Zoltana."

"The only one reporting to Zoltana was Francine Bates. She admitted yesterday she'd seen you and Rick in the hall, but I didn't get the impression it had struck her as a major event. The only man she mentioned to Zoltana was me, and only because she'd seen us leave for lunch together and assumed we were involved. It was a logical assumption. It would not have been logical to assume you and Overstreet had a secret past just because she saw you with him in the corridor at Gage and Watson."

"We do not have a secret past!"

Zac ignored the protest, using his plastic fork to break up a chunk of fried fish. "As far as I can tell, Overstreet is the only one who knew about your past relationship with him."

"But Zac, why would he use that information to blackmail me into staying out of the Zoltana case? Unless—" She broke off, shocked. "Surely you don't think he's involved—or do you?"

Zac lifted his head, munching fish. "I went to the library and checked the obit on Elena Overstreet's death. Did you know she died in a car accident? Went off the edge of the highway somewhere along the Oregon coast."

Guinevere swallowed her french fry. "No. I didn't know. Rick told me she died a couple of years ago, shortly after I stopped seeing him, but he didn't say how."

"There's more. I made a few phone calls this morning after I'd checked the old newspapers. Elena Overstreet was a very wealthy woman. Family money. Rick was the chief beneficiary in her will. When she died he became a comfortably wealthy man."

Guinevere thought of those gleaming golden eyes and shivered. Her mouth went dry. "Do you think he killed her, Zac?"

"I don't know. I talked to the cops about the accident. According to the report, there was no sign of foul play. There was a lot of fog that night, and Elena Overstreet had been drinking. Given the circumstances, her going over a cliff wasn't all that surprising."

"What was she doing driving the coastal highway? Why wasn't she on the interstate? She was a Northwest native. She wouldn't have been terribly concerned with taking the scenic route, especially at night," Guinevere noted thoughtfully.

"Mmm. The question occurred to me too. How long has Overstreet smoked those French cigarettes?"

Guinevere stared at him. "How did you know about his choice in cigarettes?"

"I carried out the trash for you the night he visited your apartment, remember? I found the butt in the garbage."

"Oh, yes. Quite the master detective, aren't you?" She didn't know whether to be annoyed or resigned. Zac hadn't said a word to her about the smell of smoke that night. He'd simply waited until disaster had struck to inform her he already knew about her visitor. There were times when Zac frightened her a little. He had a lethal sense of timing. "He was smoking them two years ago when I first met him. He still is. I don't know how long he's preferred them. Why do you ask?"

"Remember the cigarette butt we found next to Zoltana's floor safe?"

Guinevere's stomach went tight. "I remember." She waited for the punch line, knowing already what it would be.

"It was the same French brand that Overstreet smokes. I didn't check the contents of her ashtrays that night. They might have all contained that brand. Who knows? It could be a coincidence. She might just happen to prefer the same brand as Overstreet. But I don't think it's very likely."

Guinevere absorbed that information for a long moment. "But Zac, what can it possibly mean?"

"It means I think we should take another look around Madame Zoltana's this evening. If nothing else, we can verify what type of cigarette she smokes. I should have done that last time. There are other things I want to check too."

"We've already been through her house."

"I think we missed something," he said calmly, forking up the last of his fish.

"What makes you think that?"

He shrugged. "I don't know. A hunch."

She nodded, knowing better than to argue with him about one of his hunches. She had learned to respect them. "All right. What time shall we go? Midnight again?"

"That should be about right."

138

Guinevere sat watching him polish off his french fries and wondered if Zac's hunches were becoming contagious. She suddenly had the same need to take another look around Zoltana's house.

At five minutes to twelve Zac again picked the lock on the back door of Zoltana's small cottage. The door opened, and Zac and Guinevere stepped over the threshold.

There was no sign that anything had been touched since their last midnight visit. Cautiously they walked through the house, using Zac's slender flashlight.

"We know someone must have used the typewriter since we were last in here," Guinevere said as they moved into the bedroom.

"True, but if he was careful there wouldn't be any evidence. I doubt he'd be stupid enough to leave prints." Zac played the light over the desk and started opening drawers.

"Zac, what exactly are we looking for? Surely the important stuff was in Zoltana's safe, and if she was killed, the killer has whatever she was hiding."

"I think the client files were in that safe, but I don't think the heavy-duty stuff was," Zac said, scanning through some notepads he'd found. "If Zoltana was into big-time blackmail, I doubt she kept her evidence in that safe."

"Why not?"

"It's too obvious, for one thing. Look how easily we found it. Floor safes are fairly common. Besides, it would make sense to keep her client files separate from the really incriminating stuff."

Guinevere opened a closet door, using her handker-

139

chief. "Maybe she put the juicy stuff in a safe-deposit box at the bank."

"Maybe, but I doubt it. I don't think she was the type. Besides, blackmailers usually keep the evidence close at hand."

"Why?"

"Beats me. I told you, blackmail is an emotional business—on both sides. The blackmailer knows his or her life is probably only as safe as the evidence being used against the victim. There's an emotional need to keep that evidence under tight wraps, where it can be checked frequently. Blackmail is also very illegal, remember? The blackmailer prefers not to involve the establishment or the authorities in any way, so it makes sense to stay clear of banks. Too much chance of being observed. On top of everything else, Francine told us Madame Zoltana was a very private, almost housebound person. My guess is, she hid her evidence here in the house, and I don't think the blackmailer found it after he killed her. If he had found it and destroyed it, he probably wouldn't have sent you the faked pictures and the note telling you to stay out of the mess."

"I don't know, Zac, it just doesn't make a lot of sense. If Rick did kill his wife, how on earth would Madame Zoltana know about it? And what evidence could she possibly have had? For Pete's sake, we don't even know that she's dead, or that Rick was responsible, if she is."

"Right now it's all guesswork. If we can find the blackmail evidence, we'll have something to go on."

Guinevere closed the closet door with sudden decision. "The most important room in this house is Madame Zoltana's contemplation room."

Zac was crouched beside the desk, checking the back of a drawer. He looked up and met Guinevere's eyes. "A good point."

"But we already found her secret safe in there," Guinevere felt obliged to note. "How much could be hidden in that room?"

"Why don't we find out?"

He got to his feet and led the way back down the hall, coming to a halt in the doorway of the contemplation room. He shone the light around the gloomy interior.

"What about the walls?" Guinevere asked, running her fingertips along the surface of one wall.

"I don't think so. Not easily accessible. She would have had to tear up the wall every time she wanted to check her evidence. And she would have checked the evidence frequently, just to make sure it was safe."

"Another floor safe?"

"Possible, but not likely."

Guinevere glanced around the room. Her eyes fell on the crystal bowl in the center of the table. A thought occurred to her, and she went forward slowly, staring down into the bowl. "Francine said something," she murmured. "Remember? Something about Zoltana saying she looked into her own future every time she gazed into the crystal bowl?"

Zac froze, his eyes on Guinevere's profile as she stood looking at the bowl. "Lady, there are times when I think you might have missed your calling." He strode forward and used a cloth to lift the crystal bowl aside. There was a small panel of not quite opaque plastic in the table on which the bowl had sat. Zac pressed it gingerly, but nothing happened. Then he went down on one knee, shining the flashlight up under the table.

Guinevere crouched beside him as he reached up to trace a faint line in the wooden undersurface. She recalled the small, hidden drawer he had noted on their last visit. For a few minutes nothing happened, but then Zac let out a soft, satisfied exclamation as something gave. An instant later Guinevere was gazing up into a small hidden compartment. There was a tiny battery-powered light bulb inside. There was also a small package wrapped in a plastic sandwich bag.

"So that's how she made the bowl glow," Guinevere observed as Zac removed the package. "A light bulb, just as you guessed."

"Uh-huh." Zac sat cross-legged on the carpet and focused the flashlight on the plastic bag. "Too bad I didn't have enough sense to keep making guesses when I was hot. I should have checked the table the last time I was here."

Guinevere leaned forward on her knees and read the gold embossed letters on the leather book in the bag. "It's a diary."

Zac peeled open the bag and pulled out the small book. He flipped it open to the first page. "Elena Overstreet," he read.

Guinevere got to her feet. "Let's get out of here. I don't want to read that diary in this house."

He didn't argue, merely looked at her curiously for a few seconds and nodded. "We'll take it back to your apartment."

Back at her apartment Guinevere practically ran up the stairs, carrying the diary in both hands. As soon as Zac had opened the door she headed straight for the kitchen and opened the little book on the table.

"What do you think it's all about, Zac?"

"Calm down and we'll find out." He pulled the book toward him as he sat down. Guinevere leaned forward, craning her neck to read the fine, feminine hand.

The diary dated from three years previously. The last date was August fourteenth, two years earlier.

"She died August seventeenth, according to the newspapers," Zac said as he scanned the last entry first.

Guinevere stared as a familiar name leapt off one of the pages. "Look! There's a reference to Madame Zoltana. Damn, I wish Elena's handwriting was easier to read. Go back a few pages, Zac. I want to see where Madame Zoltana first appears."

Zac obediently flipped through the pages. Zoltana's name first occurred some six months before Elena's death.

It is clear the woman has a genuine talent. At our first session she demonstrated her abilities beyond a shadow of a doubt. She knew how unhappy I am and how fearful I have become lately. Unlike Dr. Stevens, she doesn't try to tell me it's all in my head, and then write out a prescription for more pills. Madame Zoltana is a great comfort to me. I fully intend to make another appointment. I am not going to tell Rick about her. He would only ridicule me, and I can't take any more of his mockery.

Guinevere sucked in her breath. "So Madame Zoltana was Elena's psychic counselor during those months before her death."

"Looks like it." Zac turned a few more pages, reading quickly. "Elena Overstreet was one scared woman, Gwen. Listen to this."

I can't shake the feeling of foreboding. I talked to Madame Zoltana about it again yesterday, and she told me that she sees a great darkness on my horizon. I told her about my panic attacks in the middle of the night, and she said they were meant as warnings. She is hoping that if she sees me on a frequent basis she will be able to determine the nature of the warnings. I am going back to her again tomorrow. Rick is not home tonight. No doubt he is out with another of his whores.

Guinevere winced as she read the last line. "It wasn't me," she told Zac defensively. "I didn't even meet him until a month after that."

"And you were never one of his whores, so relax," Zac said grimly.

"I think I'm going to feel guilty when this is all over," Guinevere said sadly.

"Why? When you were seeing Rick, you didn't even know Elena existed."

"That's true."

"And when you found out about her, you told Overstreet to take a flying leap."

Guinevere nodded again, mutely seeking reassurance.

"So stop making guilty noises and help me figure out what's going on in this diary."

His utter lack of patience with her attack of guilt made Guinevere smile in spite of herself. "That's what I like about you, Zac. You're so straightforward about life's little problems."

"I do make an effort not to let them bend my brain into spaghetti, unlike some people I could mention," he retorted dryly. "Ah, here we go, another entry mentioning Rick."

If I tell anyone about what happened last night I know I will be told I'm mentally ill. Perhaps they will send me back to the hospital. I couldn't stand that. No one but Zoltana believes me. I know Rick tried to kill me last night. All those pills he insisted I take, and then the alcohol he encouraged me to drink. I know he wanted me to overdose. Thank God I had the sense not to swallow the pills. He must have been amazed when I appeared at breakfast this morning.

"She thought he was trying to kill her, Zac!"

"It gets worse."

Together they pored over the diary, following Elena's heart-wrenching story. The woman had been terrified of reporting her fears to anyone but Zoltana, apparently because Elena had had a history of psychological problems. Eventually Zoltana became her confidant, and it was obvious Zoltana had made the most out of the situation. Toward the end of the diary Elena was visiting Zoltana three or four times a week, while Rick was at work. She never told her husband of the psychic counseling sessions.

There were two more incidents in the diary that Elena reported as attempts on her life. Both would have looked like accidents or suicide if they had succeeded. By the next to the last entry it was obvious that Elena was nearly hysterical with fear.

I don't think I will live out the week. Rick is a total stranger to me now. Perhaps he always was. I have never been so terrified in my life. I think he bought a gun yesterday. Perhaps he has given up trying to make my death appear to be a suicide. I must get out of this house. I have made up my mind. There is no one who will believe me or shelter me except Zoltana. I cannot ask her to take the risk of offering shelter. If Rick discovered I was hiding with her he would surely kill her too. No, I must go off by myself and hide. I have taken money out of the bank and I have the keys to the car. Rick had hidden them, but I found them anyway. I will leave this diary with Zoltana, along with my written request that any accident I appear to suffer be investigated as a possible case of homicide. I will instruct her that if anything should happen to me, she is to turn the diary and my request over to the police. Heaven help me, I should have left long ago. But perhaps there never was a time when I would have been safe. From the moment Rick married me, I have been his victim. He has watched me as a cat watches a mouse, waiting to pounce.

There was a handwritten note folded up in the back of the diary. A neat, formal little request from Elena Overstreet to the authorities. Guinevere's eyes burned when she read it. "That poor woman," she breathed.

Zac closed the diary. "Well, it's obvious she didn't make the best possible choice of confidants when she picked Madame Zoltana. Zoltana took her for a ride as long as she was alive, and after Elena died, she decided to go big time and blackmail Rick Overstreet. I think we can guess what finally happened to Madame Zoltana."

"I wonder how Rick found out she was the blackmailer."

"Any number of ways. Given enough time, Zoltana probably would have made a few slips and exposed herself. Once Overstreet knew who she was and what she had on him, she didn't stand a chance." Zac tapped the small book against the tabletop, his eyes unreadable. "The problem is that Overstreet can't relax completely, even if he has gotten rid of Zoltana."

"Because he didn't find the diary," Guinevere concluded.

"Exactly. He must have emptied out the safe that night and assumed he'd found what he needed. But all he got were the client files."

"This diary is not going to be enough to convict him of murder, Zac. There's no proof here, only his poor wife's fears and suspicions."

"True, but there's enough to put him in a very untenable position, and probably enough to reopen the investigation of Elena's accident. No telling where that might lead. Furthermore, we've got a missing person on our hands and more than enough evidence to send the police to Overstreet asking pointed questions."

"You know what really worries me?" Guinevere asked quietly.

"What?"

"Francine Bates. Zac, if Rick didn't find this diary the night he ransacked the safe, he's bound to wonder where it went. And if he ever figures out that Francine was Zoltana's inside person at Gage and Watson, he'll assume she has the diary."

"I know," Zac said simply. He reached for the phone and dug his notebook out of his pocket.

"What are you going to do?"

"Tell Francine and her sister to take a short vacation until I can convince the authorities to look into this. That's going to take some doing, and I'd just as soon the Bates sisters were staying anonymously in a hotel. If we found them, Overstreet could find them."

"He'd have to figure out first that Francine was involved with Zoltana."

"That's not so difficult to figure out, Gwen."

"You're right. Even I did it." She waited anxiously while Zac dialed the Bates cottage on the coast. After a few minutes it was obvious there wasn't going to be an answer. Zac hung up with a grim expression.

"Maybe they're not home."

"I think it's more likely they still aren't answering the phone. They're scared, remember."

A new level of alarm flared in Guinevere. "Zac, we've got to warn them."

He eyed her. "The only way to do that is to drive over to the coast."

"I know."

148

"We're talking a two-and-a-half-hour drive, and it's already twelve thirty."

"I know," Guinevere said again.

There was silence in the kitchen while Zac and Guinevere sat looking at each other. Then Zac got to his feet.

"Right," he said decisively. "Let's get going."

The drive to the coast seemed endless, although in truth Zac made excellent time on the empty highway. Fifty miles out of Seattle it became obvious there was a storm brewing. By the time they neared the ocean it had arrived in full force.

"Thank heavens we didn't have this rain to drive through until the last few miles," Guinevere remarked as Zac turned on the windshield wipers. "It would have slowed us down."

"Let's just hope the whole damn trip hasn't been wasted."

She gave him an alarmed glance. "What do you mean? You don't think anything has happened to Francine and Denise, do you?"

He exhaled patiently. "I only meant I hope they really are in that cottage and not out for the evening visiting friends or something. Be just our luck to make this drive when a phone call in the morning might have been all that was needed."

"I would have been a nervous wreck by morning," Guinevere told him.

"Theoretically, they aren't in any more danger now than they have been for the past few days."

"Except that Rick might be closing in on Francine." Guinevere chewed her lower lip. "I just hope he doesn't figure out her connection to Madame Zoltana too quickly."

Zac slowed for the turnoff to the Bates cottage. It was nearly three o'clock in the morning, and the lights were off in the house.

"They're probably in bed," Guinevere said reasonably.

"Probably."

"So why am I so jumpy all of a sudden?"

Zac gave her a faint smile as he parked the car. "Damned if I know. I was hoping you could tell me why I'm so jumpy."

"You're never jumpy," she accused him, holding her purse up to shield herself from the rain as she got out of the car. "You're always cool, calm, and collected. I don't know how you do it."

"Vitamins. Ready?"

"Wish you kept an umbrella in the trunk," Guinevere muttered as she hastened after him.

"Seattlelites don't carry umbrellas."

"A myth." She ducked under the shelter of the porch and brushed rain from her leather purse as Zac rang the doorbell. When there was no response he tried pounding heavily. Guinevere frowned. "They might be afraid of anyone coming to the door at this time of night. Perhaps they're playing possum."

"Miss Bates!" Zac shouted through the door. "It's Zac and Gwen. We have to talk to you."

"Open the door, Zac." Guinevere was compelled by a fierce sense of urgency. Apparently Zac was feeling the same force.

"It's open," he said, shoving at the door.

150

"Don't waste your time," Rick Overstreet said from the far end of the porch. "They're not home."

Guinevere whirled around to see him step out of the shadows, an ugly, snub-nosed gun in his hand.

"Zac!"

Zac didn't bother to answer. His hand closed around her wrist and he yanked her forward into the house, slamming the door behind them. A shot cracked viciously as the door shut, the bullet slicing through the air where Guinevere had been standing a second earlier.

Chapter Nine

Guinevere got only a brief view of the dark living room and kitchen of the cottage as Zac raced her through both rooms, but they appeared empty. There was no sign of either Bates sister.

"Zac, what are we going to do?"

"The woods out back," he bit off, yanking her through the kitchen. "With any luck, Overstreet will think we're hiding in the house, at least for a few minutes. That might give us some time. Why is that goddamn Beretta of mine always stuck under the sink in my apartment when I need it most?"

Guinevere didn't argue, as he paused for a second to open the back door and glance outside. The rain was coming down in thick, heavy torrents now. The endless dull pounding of it was a blessing, as far as Guinevere was concerned. The sound masked their movements through the house. The oppressive darkness visible through the back door offered a haven. Guinevere plunged into it without any hesitation. She had no desire to huddle under a bed inside the house waiting for Rick Overstreet to hunt down his quarry. She'd had one, horrifying glimpse into his face out there on the porch, and she knew without a shadow of a doubt that Rick had murder in mind.

"It won't take him long to figure out we're not hiding in the house," Zac said as they plunged into the heavily wooded area.

"The car . . . ?" Guinevere's breath was coming quickly already. The wet undergrowth slapped and clawed at her jeaned legs. She didn't know how far she could run, although being pursued by a man with a gun was probably going to be an excellent incentive.

In the wet darkness Zac shook his head. "The area around it is too open. No cover. We'd never make it if he spotted us. Our best bet is to draw him as far as we can into these trees."

"And then what?" Guinevere gasped.

"Then we do something real clever."

"Like what?"

"I'll let you know as soon as I think of it. Come on, behind those bushes."

"I think those are blackberry bushes, Zac. Be careful. Full of thorns."

Zac dodged around the edge of the looming clump of bushes and Guinevere followed. Her wrist was getting sore from the relentless pressure Zac was exerting on it. She didn't complain.

"You think he'll come after us?" she asked, glancing back over her shoulder. She could see little in the darkness. The dark bulk of the house was a featureless blot barely visible between the trees.

"He'll come after us." Zac sounded grimly certain. "He has to come after us. He's got too much at stake. We know who he is and what he's done. He can't afford to let us get away."

"Somehow," Guinevere muttered dismally, "I didn't expect my big case to end quite this way."

"Neither did I. Life with you is full of surprises, Gwen." The observation was clearly not meant as a compliment.

A harsh, cracking sound echoed through the rain. Guinevere gulped air. "Zac!"

"He's shooting blindly. He can't possibly see us."

"Zac, I saw a light," Guinevere whispered after another quick glance over her shoulder. "He's got a big flashlight."

"Well, at least we'll always know right where he is, won't we? That flashlight will act as a beacon."

"I love the way you always look on the bright side."

"Come on, I think this is about as far as we can go. The trees are starting to thin out again, and we need their protection. We have to stay among them." Zac slowed to a halt and tugged Guinevere to the right.

She struggled after him, her chest tight with the effort of drawing in oxygen. "If we get out of this, I think I'd better sign up for an aerobics class. No stamina."

"You're doing fine. I'm the one who'd better sign up for the class." He pushed her down behind a massive, chest-high cluster of twisted berry bushes. "Listen to me, Gwen. I want you to stay here, understand?"

Guinevere ignored the stinging in her palm as she unthinkingly closed her hand around a thorny branch. She looked up, trying to see his face in the darkness and rain. In the wet shadows she got only an impression of harsh planes and angles. His eyes seemed colorless, but the glittering intensity in them was frightening. It was the image of a face belonging to a creature that hunted and killed to survive. It crossed her mind that it was because of her that Zac had once again been transformed into this grim, relentless, very dangerous being.

"I'm sorry, Zac," she heard herself whisper, her voice a mere thread of sound.

He didn't pay any attention to the useless apology. "Don't move, Gwen."

"Yes, Zac."

He urged her down until she was crouched in the mud and then he was gone, his passage soundless in the night. Guinevere hugged herself, recovering her breath as she strained to listen. She became aware of a weight on her right shoulder and realized in vague surprise that she still had her leather bag. Amazing how strong a woman's instinct was when it came to hanging on to her purse.

Minutes passed. Guinevere could hear nothing but the endlessly thudding rain. She knew Zac was out there somewhere, hunting the man who was hunting them. Her mind conjured up a bizarre scene of two dangerous wild animals prowling through the night, seeking each other's throats. She thought of Rick Overstreet's golden cat's eyes, and of Zac's strong, quiet strength.

Another shot cracked through the trees. Instinctively, Guinevere ducked, although she knew Rick couldn't possibly see her. The strain of waiting behind the berry bushes was quickly eating at her nerves, though. She needed to know where Overstreet was.

She crawled through the mud on her hands and knees, peering around the edge of the berry thicket. For a moment she could see nothing, and then Rick's flashlight cut a vicious swath through the night. She froze, trying to spot Zac and wondering how long it would take Rick to find Zac's hiding place, or her own.

When the light shifted in another direction Guinevere caught an impression of movement to her left and realized it was probably Zac. She narrowed her eyes, struggling to see through the pouring rain, and decided he was working his way around an invisible circle that would ultimately bring him to a point directly across from her.

It made sense from his viewpoint, she realized. He would be able to keep an eye on her location and make sure Overstreet didn't find her first. He would also be able to track Rick's progress through the woods. But as far as Guinevere could tell, the only action Zac would be able to take would be to leap out and try to take Rick by surprise. She shuddered. Rick had a gun and a flashlight. It was going to be damn risky.

Minutes slipped past. Guinevere was soaked and she was getting chilled, but still she crouched where Zac had left her. The slanting flashlight beam kept cutting through the night in a pattern that indicated Rick was methodically searching every inch of the wooded terrain. He must have realized that Zac was unarmed.

Guinevere flinched as the flashlight began moving closer. Zac was right. In one respect the light made it easy to keep tabs on Rick. But there was a certain horrifying inevitability about its movement. Given enough time, Rick was sure to find one or both of them. Guinevere huddled more tightly into herself, watching the flashlight through the twisted berry vines. She was soaking wet.

"You should never have gotten involved, Gwen."

Rick's voice shocked her. For some reason, she

hadn't expected him to start talking. He must be feeling very confident. Or perhaps he thought he could rattle her and Zac.

"What made you do it? How did you figure out that that Zoltana bitch was blackmailing me? It was a mistake to drag your lover into this. I'm going to have to kill you both now. You know that, don't you? And when I'm done with you two, I'll take care of that goddamn Francine Bates. Zoltana gave that stupid diary to her, didn't she? It's the only explanation. It took me a while to put it all together. I didn't realize the Bates woman was connected with Zoltana until today, when I had a talk with one of your silly little temps at work. She let it slip, and then I realized what must have happened to Elena's diary. But I can't figure you out, Gwen, or that bastard with you. How the hell did you get involved?"

Rick was edging closer, the flashlight still moving in sweeping arcs. Overstreet was only a dark, lethal shadow behind the glare of the light. Guinevere wished she could make herself smaller. The temptation to break and run was almost overwhelming, but instinct warned her that that would be stupid. Rick was too close now. He would detect the movement. Her fingers closed around a rock lying in the mud beside her. It was a poor excuse for a weapon, but she didn't have anything else. Guinevere held her breath, aware her fingers were shaking around the cold, hard rock.

She was tensing herself for a wild, desperate throw, when she realized Rick had changed direction. He was no longer coming toward her berry-bush cover. The flashlight was moving toward a point diametrically across from her. It was the direction in which Zac had disappeared.

Guinevere moved her head slightly, trying to follow the beam of light. It glanced off several trees and then skimmed over a small, tumbled pile of rocks. It froze on the rocks, and Guinevere knew for certain Rick had found Zac's hiding place. What's more, she knew Rick had realized the same thing. The light didn't shift from the rocks.

"Come on out and I'll make it quick and clean," Rick promised with a hungry anticipation that went well with his catlike eyes. "I want to get this over with. Come on," he urged, moving slowly toward the jumble of granite. *"Come on!"*

Zac didn't stand a chance. His hiding place was exposed in the full glare of the flashlight. The most he could hope to do was make a break for it, and Guinevere knew he'd never make it. Rick would cut him down in a split second. Fury overwhelmed her. She was on her feet before she had time to think, heaving the shoulder bag uselessly in Rick's direction. It fell short but it brought Rick around with jolting swiftness, the flashlight blinding her.

"You bastard!" she yelled, and then dove for the mud as Rick lifted the gun. A shot slammed through the berry bushes above her head and the flashlight swung wildly, as though Rick had staggered. She flattened herself, waiting for the next shot, but it never came. Instead there was a shout of rage from Rick Overstreet and the unmistakable sound of bodies hitting the ground.

Guinevere jerked to her feet, knowing Zac must have jumped the other man. The flashlight lay on the soggy ground, its steady beam revealing a twisting flurry of arms and legs. Guinevere raced forward, but she knew even before she reached the light that Zac had everything under control. She was in time to see the final, savage blows, as he straddled Overstreet and slammed his fist against Rick's jaw. Overstreet went abruptly still.

"Zac! Are you all right?" Guinevere scrambled for the flashlight, aiming it at his face. Blood glinted on his mouth. In that instant he was the hunter who had made his kill. In the brilliant glare of the flashlight his eyes were pools of slowly retreating menace.

"I'm fine. Would you kindly stop trying to blind me with that goddamn flashlight?"

"Oh, sorry." Hastily she swerved the light out of his eyes and aimed it at Overstreet. There was considerably more blood on Rick's handsome features than there was on Zac's face. "I was scared to death."

"Not half as scared as I was when you stood up and threw that stupid purse at him," Zac muttered, reaching for the gun, which had fallen into the mud. He climbed to his feet. "What the hell did you think you were doing? I thought I told you to stay behind those bushes."

"He had you pinned behind those rocks. He was going to kill you!"

"I wasn't behind the rocks," Zac said mildly, watching her. "I was over there behind those trees. That pile of rocks was a little too obvious."

Guinevere stared at him. "You weren't behind the rocks? But I was sure I'd seen you disappear in this direction."

"We can discuss this at some other time. Not now. Help me get this bastard back to the house."

Guinevere bit her lip at the disgusted anger in his voice. It was obvious Zac was not in a cheerful mood. She could hardly blame him. Silently she bent to grab one of Rick's limp arms.

It was six o'clock in the morning before Guinevere and Zac finally checked in to a small beachfront motel. The desk clerk had taken one look at Zac's bruised face and cold eyes and hadn't argued about the fact that his new guests had neither luggage nor a semblance of respectability. He pointedly pretended to ignore Guinevere's disreputable appearance. Her hair was hanging in damp tendrils around her shoulders, and she was wearing an oversize shirt that had been loaned to her by a sheriff's deputy.

Zac accepted the key without a word and led the way along the second floor to the room they had been assigned.

"First, a shower." He slammed the door shut and locked it.

Guinevere didn't want to argue with him any more than the desk clerk had. Obediently she headed toward the bathroom, stripping off the borrowed shirt and the rest of her clothing as she went. Zac followed, leaving a trail of muddy clothes behind him. When she had the hot water on full blast he stepped in beside her.

Guinevere waited until she could stand it no longer. Zac had been dangerously silent too long. The only real talking he had done had been to the sheriff's men, whom he had called from the Bates cottage. Clutching the bar of soap, she looked up at him through the steaming water.

"Why don't you just chew me out and get it over with? I can't stand the suspense."

He opened his eyes beneath the water and glared at her. For a moment he was silent, but there was emotion moving now in his eyes. That had to be some sort of improvement, Guinevere figured. She hated it when Zac's eyes went cold.

"You little fool. You almost got yourself killed." He didn't touch her, but Guinevere got the impression that was because he didn't quite trust himself to touch her.

"Zac, I've already apologized for that scene back in the woods. I told you, I thought Rick had found your hiding place. How was I to know you weren't behind those rocks? It was a logical place to hide." Her eyes widened slightly. "Which was exactly what you wanted Rick to think, didn't you? You were going to jump him from behind when he tried to flush you out from the cover of the rocks."

"That was the general idea," Zac said through gritted teeth. "How was I to know you were going to pop up and start yelling and throwing purses?"

"But Zac, you've got to admit it provided a useful distraction for you," Guinevere said logically. "Who knows? You might not have gotten a good chance at Rick otherwise."

"That is not the point, Gwen." He put his big hands on her bare shoulders and brought her close. "The point is that you risked your neck out there, after I had given you strict orders to stay down and keep out of sight."

"Yes, well, I felt I had to improvise. And it worked, Zac. You got a clear shot at him. Admit it. Admit my causing that distraction was very useful for you."

"I'll admit nothing of the kind. I ought to turn you over my knee."

She grinned, relaxing slightly as she sensed some of the tension draining from him at last. She put her arms around his neck and let the tips of her breasts brush his chest. "How long have you had this kinky streak in you?"

Zac groaned and pulled her closer. "If I weren't so damn tired I'd do it, you know. But somehow, after that little game of hide-and-seek in the woods, plus two hours of talking myself hoarse trying to explain this mess to the authorities, I find my reserves of energy are totally depleted. Turn off the water and let's go to bed, Gwen. We both need some sleep before we drive back to Seattle. I'll finish yelling at you later."

"Whatever you say, Zac." She turned off the taps and reached for a towel.

Twenty minutes later they collapsed side by side beneath the covers, the drapes firmly pulled against the early morning light. A waiting silence hung over the bed for a few minutes, and then Zac tucked Guinevere against him, his leg settling with possessive intimacy over hers.

"Gwen?"

"Hmm?"

"You probably saved our lives back there in the woods."

Guinevere's lashes lifted. "What?"

He sighed and settled her closer. "You were right.

162

The distraction you caused bought me the time I needed."

"Oh, Zac . . ."

"I don't want to think about how many years it took off my life, however," he concluded.

"I wouldn't worry about it," she smiled. "You're in great shape."

There was another stretch of silence, and then Zac spoke again, into Guinevere's ear.

"Gwen?"

"Hmm?"

"It turns out I'm not sleepy. Too much adrenaline, I guess."

"That's too bad, seeing as how you've already charged this room to your corporate account," she reminded him regretfully. "You're going to have to pay for it whether we use it or not."

"We can always put the bed to another use." His palm closed possessively over her breast as he nuzzled the sensitive place behind her ear.

Guinevere sighed contentedly. "Yes, I suppose we could. Waste not, want not."

Zac pushed her back against the mattress. Then he came down on top of her with a sudden urgency that whipped the banked fires of her own sensuality into a glowing blaze. They made love until the jagged edges of the night's danger and terror were dulled, and then finally they slept.

Three days later Guinevere stood in the center of Zac's new office suite talking to Sally Evenson and Evelyn Pemberton. She was entertaining them with the details of the Zoltana case, while Zac worked himself into a frenzy of anxiety and party-giver's panic. Periodically he moved through the room, double-checking the position of the caterer's platters. Then he disappeared into the second office to count champagne glasses. The reception was due to start in fifteen minutes and Zac had convinced himself that no one would appear.

"Zoltana had been running her little con game for years," Guinevere explained to Sally, who listened with avid attention. Sally was wearing her royal blue blazer tonight and was thrilled to have been invited as one of Zac's clients, even though she didn't pay one penny of Zac's usually hefty fees for his services. Sally was unique in that she had gotten his help for free. Still, ultimately she had been a client, and as such she deserved an invitation to the evening's festivities.

Evelyn Pemberton nodded, one eye on Zac, who was adjusting a canapé tray for the tenth time. "I can understand how it would work. She gave her clients the impression she really could read their past and guide them in making decisions about the future. Then the susceptible ones kept coming back for more. A nice steady income."

Sally sighed. "She could be very persuasive."

"I don't doubt it," Guinevere agreed. "She certainly had Elena Overstreet on a string. The poor woman latched onto Madame Zoltana and clung to her. Zoltana fed her fears, the way she normally did, probably assuming they were false. It undoubtedly came as a shock when Elena died. There sat Zoltana with the incriminating diary and enough knowledge to guess what might have happened. She hesitated for several months, but then she contacted Rick Overstreet anonymously and let him know her silence could be bought for a price. For a while she got away with it."

"How did he find out she was the blackmailer?" Evelyn Pemberton asked. She swung around suddenly. "Mr. Justis, please don't worry about that canapé tray. It's perfect the way it is."

"I was just straightening it," he muttered, stalking into the other office.

"According to the cops, Rick finally tracked Zoltana down by keeping an eye on the drop point she chose for the payoffs. It wasn't easy, because she changed the points constantly, and Rick couldn't take long hours off from work to watch bus depot lockers and private post office boxes all day long. But one day a couple of months ago he got lucky."

"Then he set about planning to kill her." Sally shuddered.

"He took his time about planning her death. He still hasn't admitted he did it. But the police said a Jane Doe that fit the description of Madame Zoltana turned up in Lake Washington last week. They think they can tie Rick to it. If nothing else, they've got him for attempted murder," Guinevere said.

"Attempted murder of you and Zac," Evelyn Pemberton said, shaking her head. "What about Francine Bates and her sister?" Before Guinevere could answer, Evelyn called through the doorway into the next office, "Mr. Justis, don't touch the glasses. You'll get fingerprints on them. Just let the caterer's staff handle things. That's what they're here for."

Guinevere hid a grin as Zac reluctantly refrained from picking up one of the glasses that sat on his desk in the second office. He paced restlessly back out into the main room, straightening his already straight tie. He answered Evelyn's question. "Before he killed Zoltana, Rick forced her to reveal the safe. She kept quiet about the other hiding place, hoping to use it to bargain for her life. He grabbed the contents of the safe without looking at them, assumed he had what he needed, and shot Zoltana before she could convince him there was a second hiding place. Then he dumped her body in the lake, knowing it was going to take a long time before anyone reported her missing. It was only later that he realized he didn't have the evidence against himself that he'd gone after. But he was a greedy man. He couldn't resist trying to squeeze some easy money out of Zoltana's victims, so he sent a note to Sally and some of the others. In the meantime, he kept wondering what had happened to the diary."

Zac reached the far end of the room and spun around, pacing back past Guinevere and the other two women. "He also decided to make a pass at Gwen. He went over to her apartment one evening and saw the note he'd sent to Sally, the one he'd signed with Zoltana's name. It was lying right out there in the open on a table. He also saw the note Gwen and I typed on Zoltana's typewriter. At that point he knew he had real trouble. Gwen was obviously asking questions about Madame Zoltana, and that was dangerous for him."

"I see," Evelyn Pemberton said slowly. "But he assumed you didn't know anything about the diary."

"True, and at that point we didn't," Guinevere agreed, knowing neither she nor Zac intended to talk about Rick's blackmail attempt. Overstreet had originally prepared the photos intending to use them to coerce Guinevere into going to bed with him. But after he'd seen the notes, he'd used the doctored pictures in an attempt to scare her off the case instead. "He was, however, holding all the client data he'd taken from the safe. He also had a list of payoffs to Zoltana's inside person at Gage and Watson, although she hadn't put down Francine Bates's name, thank heaven. It gave poor Francine some time. But eventually Rick figured out what the record of payments was, and then he decided to get rid of Francine on the assumption that she knew too much. She might also have the diary. It was logical that Zoltana might have told her about it."

Sally's eyes widened. "But then you found the diary, and decided to warn poor Francine she might be in great danger."

Zac whipped around from the other side of the room, glancing at his watch. "But Francine had gotten nervous enough to move out of the cottage and take her sister with her. When Gwen and I found her, she realized the murderer could too. So she and Denise headed for Oregon. The cops located them yesterday, and told them they had Overstreet in custody. Where the hell is everyone?"

"It's only five forty-five, Zac," Mrs. Pemberton said firmly. "Relax."

He ran a finger around his collar and glared at Guinevere. "If no one shows up I'm holding you personally responsible. This was all your idea. You said it would be good public relations."

"Calm down, Zac. Everything's going to be fine," Guinevere soothed gently, aware that her eyes were undoubtedly mirroring her amusement.

Sally Evenson finished the tale. "I guess it was my fault Mr. Overstreet got the final bit of information he needed to know Francine was involved. He stopped me in the hall yesterday and asked me all sorts of questions."

"He knew you were one of Zoltana's victims," Zac pointed out. "And he was blackmailing you himself. It was logical you might be able to tell him who the inside person was, even if you didn't realize you knew. He was fishing for information."

"I didn't understand what he was asking," Sally explained unhappily. "He just started talking about Francine and a few of the other women in the office. I answered his questions, and I guess I told him something that pinpointed Francine. Thank heaven she wasn't at the cottage when Rick arrived."

"Yes," responded Zac dryly. "Unfortunately, not all of us were quite that lucky." He shot a baleful glance at Guinevere.

Before Guinevere could respond, a voice hailed them from the open doorway.

"Hey, is this the office where the free food is supposed to be?" Mason Adair, the artist, sauntered into the room, Guinevere's sister Carla on his arm. Both were smiling broadly. "Nice spread, Zac. I suppose we have to wait until the big-time clients arrive before we tear it apart?"

Zac was visibly relieved that someone had shown up after all. "Help yourself. How are you, Mason?"

"Doing great, thanks. Carla here has my career well in hand." He glanced at the canvases on the walls. "Glad you like the pictures."

"They look terrific in here," Carla observed. "But then, they would, of course. A Mason Adair picture is an asset to any important room."

Zac was nodding his head in willing agreement when another couple appeared in the doorway.

"Good evening, Zac. Are we on time?"

Zac grinned. "Come on in. Evelyn, this is Edward Vandyke and his wife. Mr. Vandyke is a former client of mine. Mr. and Mrs. Vandyke, this is my new executive secretary, Evelyn Pemberton."

"How do you do, Mrs. Pemberton?" Mrs. Vandyke said with a warm smile. "I'm sure you'll find working with Zac very interesting." She turned to Guinevere. "Good to see you again. How is the temporary service business doing?"

Guinevere responded to the easy inquiry as someone else walked into the room. Out of the corner of her eye she watched the trickle turn into a rush, and within half an hour the small suite was crowded with people. Zac was the perfect host, relaxing finally, as it became obvious the reception was not going to be a social disaster. Guinevere found him alone for a moment in the inner office, where he had gone to bring out more champagne. She cornered him at the desk and held out her glass for a refill.

"Congratulations, Mr. Justis. You're a success."

His gray eyes gleamed as he looked down at her. "Thanks to you. I couldn't have done it without you, Gwen. I'll admit it."

"My tab is paid for your services on the Zoltana case, then?"

"We can discuss what you still owe tonight after we get home," he returned smoothly.

Her mouth curved. "Home," she repeated. "I like the sound of that."

"So do I. It strikes me that maintaining two apartments has become an unnecessary expense. What do you think?" There was a sudden, curious tension in him, although his voice was casual.

"I think so too," she agreed softly.

He bent his head and kissed her briefly, his mouth warm with promise.

"Did I ever tell you what Madame Zoltana said about you the day I went to see her?" Guinevere asked musingly as Zac raised his head.

"I don't believe you went into great detail."

"She said you were a good lover."

"Ah," said Zac complacently. "I always knew the woman had a certain amount of true psychic ability."

"Yes," said Guinevere, remembering the events of the past few days. "I think she did."

 COMING IN MARCH

TOUCHSTONE

Margaret Dobson

Read this exciting excerpt
from the first of the
JANE BAILEY NOVELS!

Dear Jane:

*Look at the HONCC and think of a(n) STOREY.
But just remember, when you've got it, you won't
really have it at all. Because it isn't there. Still, don't
let anyone take it away from you.*

*Love,
Ted*

*P.S. Hope this riddle is right up your armchair-
sleuthing alley. So much for fun. In the end,
you'll find the combs more useful. Soon.*

Jane smoothed the note out on her vanity table and
sat back to stare at the box that held a pink conch
shell and two flamboyant cloisonné combs shaped like
colorful peacock tails. The now familiar tightness in
her chest returned.

This was her brother, she mused. Not the watch.
Not the wallet. Not the clothes. Not any of the personal effects she'd received the day before the funeral.
This package, cryptic message and all, was his legacy.
It signified the brother she had always known. Ted,
the gift-giver. Ted, the good-natured tease. The one
who was thoughtful. The one who humored her love
of a mystery. The one who was invariably late.

173

Her mouth puckered.

The one who wouldn't be there anymore.

She wiped away her tears and breathed deeply. Enough was enough, already.

Even Ted would agree, she reasoned, brushing a section of unruly hair before fastening one of the combs in it. She placed the second comb on the other side of her head. The result was one that pleased her, even if she did resemble a candidate for a soap commercial.

That done, Jane was drawn again to the note, which was printed in Teddy's stylish, bold lettering. She smiled. He'd stubbornly refused to learn cursive. The words in caps would of course be anagrams. He liked those. She did too. The first wasn't difficult to unscramble. *HONCC* most certainly had to be *conch*.

She looked around for a pen.

"Jane, it's almost eight thirty. We'd better be going."

Jane glanced at the bedroom door, which was slightly ajar. "I'll be ready in a few more minutes, Aunt Minnie."

Pushing thoughts of the bookstore aside, she used her sharpest eyebrow pencil to cross out the first anagram and insert *conch* above it. The second, *STOREY,* wasn't so easy. She began to play with the letters, rearranging their order. The right word would begin with a vowel, since he'd inserted the *(n)* after *a. estory. erosty. eyrsto.* No, she didn't think *e* was right. *ostery. ortsey. orstey. oyrtes. oyst . . . er. Oyster.* That was it. *Oyster.* She drew a line through *STOREY* and penciled in the new word above it.

Look at the conch and think of an oyster.

She frowned and picked up the shell, turning the

spiky form in her hands. She shook it, and heard a soft metallic tinkling sound. Oysters held only one interest for her.

Pearls! Had he sent her pearls?

She tapped the open side of the conch against her palm. Nothing. She closed one eye to peer inside. Darkness. She poked a finger in as far as it would go. She couldn't feel a thing. But there was something in there. She knew that.

Jane fumbled in a drawer for tweezers.

Alternately shaking and turning the shell, she reached inside with the tweezers. Again and again she came up empty. Finally she set the conch aside in frustration and tossed the tweezers onto the vanity.

What was she doing anyway? It was too early in the morning for games. And Aunt Minnie was waiting to go to work. But she couldn't leave now. Not without knowing what was inside that shell, for God's sake.

She lifted the conch again, turned it, shook it, reached inside it with the tweezers. Then she caught something, and coaxed whatever it was out into the open.

The sight of two lustrous beads that looked like translucent ivory made her pulse quicken. But the subsequent flash of crystal stunned her. With trembling fingers Jane gently tugged her find out of the shell.

Good God, it was diamonds and pearls. A whole string of them.

Her gaze moved along the strand of pearls to the first cluster of tiny diamonds, then on to the next group of pearls—ten or so—before another set of diamonds appeared. There were at least a dozen such clusters nestled among the pearls.

The clasp was made of gold and was shaped like a scorpion. She struggled an interminable moment to unfasten it. When the necklace rested around her neck, only then did she become aware of the pronounced rise and fall of her chest. She swallowed, looking into the oval mirror as the facets of the stones twinkled at her.

Where did Teddy get these? she wondered.

"Jane, we really should go."

The sound of Minnie's voice galvanized her into action. "Coming, Aunt Minnie. I'm coming right now."

With great care she took off the necklace, but didn't know what to do with it. Her usual hiding places seemed a bit lightweight for this piece of jewelry.

Gathering the strand of pearls and diamonds into a small but brilliant heap in her palm, she stuffed it back inside the spiraling shell, which she rotated vigorously until she could hear only the faintest tinkle.

Then Jane relaxed.

He'd probably won it gambling, she decided. That was it. Ted had gotten lucky.

The conch was a tight squeeze in the top drawer of her vanity, where it would be out of sight—but not out of mind. It was the most elegant necklace she'd ever seen. It must've cost a fortune. Ted had never come near the money needed for that. He'd rarely had enough money for plane fare home.

But she would think about all that later. Right now, the store was waiting. She would come home tonight and think this thing through. No need to worry about it now.

Jane reached for her purse and went to the door.

But where in God's name did he *get* it!

On a platform behind the old-fashioned cash register she stood a little higher than he. Phillip was forced to look up at the combs in her hair. He had spotted them almost immediately, just after the bell had clanged over the door of Bailey and Company, announcing his entrance.

"Why, hello, Phillip. How nice of you to stop by."

Jane smiled with such innocence that he wanted to shake her. She had lied to him. He supposed she *could* have received the combs months ago. But the memory of Ted Bailey browsing in an Aruban gift shop the week before his death flashed like neon through Phillip's thoughts. Still, he nodded and offered Jane a brief smile of his own.

"Afternoon, Jane. I see you've come back to work."

"Yes. Aunt Minnie and I decided it would be the best therapy."

"Good idea. It's always wise to start putting your life back on an even keel as soon as possible."

She looked away for a moment. "Yes, I think so too."

Along with a cream-colored dress, the only pieces of jewelry she wore were pearl earrings set against gold clovers—and the combs, of course.

"Your hair looks very attractive that way," he said.

Her shoulders tensed slightly. "Thank you."

"Nice combs," he said. "They look a lot like ones I've seen in Aruba."

He thought he saw her start to reach for one of them, but her fingers went instead to the pearl on her right earlobe. Then a woman and a small boy approached the counter. Phillip stepped away while Jane rang up the sale and chatted with the customer, whom she obviously knew very well. Several paperbacks and a magazine went into a crisp plastic bag printed with *Happy Reading from Bailey and Company.*

When the mother and son left, he tried to catch Jane off guard. "Did you get them here in Tulsa?" he asked.

"What?"

"The combs."

An impatient sigh escaped her. "No."

Phillip didn't leave it at that. He kept staring, remembering his mother's constant reprimands for "blatant rudeness." He'd never listened. Over the years, he'd only embellished on his bad habit by honing his ability to tip his chin admiringly, innocently, accusingly—whatever it took to get someone to talk. Sometimes it worked. Sometimes it didn't. This time it looked like it might.

Looking worried, Jane edged along the counter and stepped down from the platform. At last he had a full view of her. And a nice view it was. He rather liked her legs. Thinking it best not to let his eyes linger there, Phillip pulled his gaze back to her face. She'd begun to straighten an already neat stack of periodicals.

"You know, the funniest thing has happened," she said. "Well, not really funny, but odd. I received a small package from Teddy this morning. It was postmarked the day before he died. It felt strange to receive something from a dead—" Jane stopped herself. She looked toward him, but not at him, and shrugged helplessly. "Teddy sent me the combs."

178

She was acting defensive, nervous—and guilty, maybe? Obviously she'd avoided telling him. Why?

"Well, the postal service in the Caribbean has never been known for speed or compassion," he said. "Was there anything besides the combs in the package?"

Again she hesitated slightly. "A shell. You know, the kind probably *every* beach in Aruba is covered with."

"Actually, I didn't find many shells on the beaches. What kind of shell was it?"

"I don't know. Conch, I think. Teddy often sent trinkets like that. Souvenirs, you know. Combs and shells and—the like."

"Is that all?"

Her chin shot up. "Sometimes it was other things—"

"No, I meant is that all there was *this* time." Damn, he wished he didn't have to drag it out of her. She was beginning to get suspicious.

"The usual short note. He said he'd be returning soon."

"Did he say why? Or when exactly?"

"No." Then she broke down and smiled tenderly. "Teddy *always* said he'd be home soon. It didn't necessarily mean anything. We never looked for him until we saw him coming."

"I see. Nonetheless, it's clear that you were very close to your brother."

Keeping an eye on Jane, Phillip reached for his package of cigarettes. She tipped her head and glanced in the direction of the smoking sign, as in "thank you for not." His Winstons went back into his pocket.

"Bailey and Company thanks you, as does the fire department," she said.

He couldn't really say it was his pleasure.

"Is your aunt here?"

"She's gone home for lunch. Her apartment's just a few blocks away."

"Would you like to have lunch with me when she comes back?"

"Thanks, but she's going to bring me a sandwich."

"How about dinner?"

She frowned in indecision. "Thanks again, but I'll be having dinner with her this evening. She wants to cook something. Busywork, I guess."

"I understand. Maybe some other time. I'll just browse awhile, if you don't mind."

"Not at all. That's what we're here for."

Phillip opened a magazine and began to turn the pages. Funny, he thought. He wasn't here for that reason at all.

But just remember, when you've got it, you won't really have it at all. Because it isn't there.

But what did the message mean? She'd been thinking about it most of the afternoon and it still didn't make any sense. She *did* have it. It *was* there. In her bedroom at home.

Jane steered the car into the left lane and tried not to frown, although she doubted Aunt Minnie would notice. Her aunt seemed more interested in the scenery.

It was early evening. The joggers were out in full force in the park along Riverside Drive. The temperature had dropped and the windows were down. Aunt

Minnie had decided that cooking would make her busier than she wanted to be that evening, so they'd opted for takeout. The aromas of the Colonel's fried chicken for her aunt and the Chinese food from the Egg Roll Express for Jane mingled with a welcome cool breeze off the Arkansas.

Aunt Minnie clucked her tongue. "Just look at the shorts those women are wearing. Why, they're positively hanging out of them. And in the *daytime.*" She sighed. "But maybe I'm getting old."

"Oh, you'll never get old, Aunt Minnie."

"You're right, of course. I don't even know why I said it."

Jane's mouth curved with affection.

"Why, in some ways I'm younger than you," Aunt Minnie observed. "You ought to be out doing something like that, Jane."

"You want me to go to the park and hang out of my shorts?"

"Better than hanging out with me and a box of chicken. You might at least meet someone."

"Most likely a mugger, with my luck."

Aunt Minnie ignored her. "Someone like Phillip Decker would be nice. God, now there's a man. Tall, dark, and handsome." She frowned. "Are they still using that criteria to describe a hulk these days?"

"You mean a hunk, Aunt Minnie."

"Oh. Well, all I know is that man could charm the fuzz off a peach. And he's so *nice.*"

"I agree. He seems rather nice."

But Jane had her doubts as to just how nice he was. Since Teddy's surprise, she seemed to have doubts about everyone, including herself. Phillip Decker liked to ask questions. She got the feeling he already knew some of the answers. Yes, he *seemed* nice. He was very definitely attractive. She could even concede that he had charm. But there was one thing she couldn't concede—that he was all that he claimed to be. Phillip Decker, who'd *said* he worked in insurance, was nowhere to be found in the yellow pages. She didn't believe that he'd been all that friendly with Teddy, either. But if he hadn't been Teddy's friend, what *was* the connection between him and her brother?

"Aunt Minnie?"

"Hmm?"

"How would you feel if you learned that someone you loved wasn't . . . everything you always believed him to be?"

Aunt Minnie's head slowly turned in her direction. "Are you in love with Phillip Decker? Jane, dear, don't you think you should get to know him a little first?"

Jane sighed, and chuckled at the prospect. "No, Aunt Minnie. Someone like . . ." She drew a bolstering breath. "Someone like—Teddy, for instance."

There was a thoughtful silence before Minnie replied. "In that case, I don't think I'd want to hear about it."

That puts a slight damper on things, Jane thought. Whom else did she have to talk to?

"Jane, it isn't that I don't have great respect for the truth, mind you. But there are times when one's peace of mind is more important. Especially when the truth won't make things better. Sometimes I'd just as soon keep my head in the sand. Do you understand?"

"Yes, I think I do."

Jane parked the car across the street from Aunt Minnie's apartment complex. Carrying their respective dinners, they entered the building, and Minnie headed straight for the stairway, setting a brisk pace. Jane directed a longing glance toward the elevator and then caught up with her aunt, whose tone had become equally brisk.

"But that's just *my* way of dealing with life," Minnie was saying. "It doesn't have to be yours. Has Phillip Decker said something to make you suspicious?"

"No. Just curious."

"Hmph. If you think he knows something about your brother that you ought to know, then you should simply ask him."

"Maybe. What if he doesn't see fit to discuss it?"

"That's easy enough." Her voice echoing through the stairwell, Aunt Minnie stopped on the second-floor landing to catch her breath. "Tell him that you have an uncle—no, make that a lover—in the attorney general's office who has his eye on a Senate seat. And for God's sake, don't say it's Dennis."

"Why not?" Jane teased, knowing Aunt Minnie had never felt more than lukewarm about Dennis.

"Well, because he isn't at all . . . he's too . . ." Minnie started up the steps to the third floor. "Dennis is so . . ."

"Genteel?" Jane said behind her, her calves beginning to ache.

"Something like that. Anyway, tell Phillip Decker that your lover would be happy to make his life miserable unless he tells you what you want to know."

"So you think I should make threats," Jane said,

following her aunt into the third floor corridor. "Aunt Minnie, you're incredible."

"Yes, well, tough times call for tough talk, cookie. You'd know that if you'd ever been to a white sale. Now, would you be a dear and find my keys before I faint dead away? My feet are killing me."

Jane did as she was told. But, opening the door, she couldn't help smiling as Aunt Minnie all but swaggered past her. Head in the sand, indeed.

When the overhead light went on, Phillip's head came up. He froze for a moment, then looked at the door. Slowly, without any unnecessary moves, he eased up off the edge of Jane Bailey's bed. The room was so quiet that he thought he heard the hems of his pants hit the tops of his shoes.

Her hand slid down from the light switch. She got a good hold on the derringer and an excellent bead on him. But he knew she would have to get closer to hit him.

She took a few steps toward him.

"What are you doing here?" she asked.

Phillip hesitated, not knowing what to say. God, it was only too clear what he was doing. The damn conch lay in pieces at his feet. He had the necklace in one palm, his jeweler's loupe in the other. What more did the woman want for an explanation?

He shrugged. It seemed the only response that wouldn't appear redundant.

"Why did you break my shell?" she asked.

He would have thought the answer to that was obvious too. At the time, he'd been in one hell of a hurry, but he didn't say so. Phillip was scared. Damn scared.

But he didn't think he was half as frightened as she was, asking such rhetorical questions and all. Her hand was trembling a bit. He weighed her chances of firing the pistol, and then he weighed his chances of being shot. The odds were not in his favor.

"Why don't you say something, Decker?"

He hated it when women called him Decker. She wasn't Ma Barker, for God's sake. If she was going to shoot him, couldn't she just be herself instead of some tough-talking mama?

"It's difficult to think with that gun pointed at me," he said.

"Well, you'd better get used to it, because it isn't going anywhere. Now, I want you to walk very slowly to the vanity and put *my* necklace down."

Phillip did as he was told. As soon as the necklace was out of his hands, she nodded.

"Now, go back to where you were," she said.

He did that too.

She stepped warily toward the necklace, snatched it up, and almost skittered back to her place near the door. She was petrified, afraid to get anywhere near him. He began to wonder if the gun was even loaded. Even so, he couldn't be blasé. He'd have to tread lightly.

"Do you always keep a gun in the house?" he asked.

"Always."

"I see. It holds two shells, doesn't it?"

She raised her chin. "Just never you mind how many. I've got plenty more ammo where this came from."

Ammo, he thought. How quaint. "What kind of—ammo?"

"Twenty-two magnum."

"Oh." He took a step back.

"Is that good?"

He swallowed. "An excellent choice. You could do a lot of damage. But you wouldn't really—"

"You bet I would." She seemed to regain her confidence. "After all, if a woman's gonna pack a . . . rod, she damn sure better be willing to use it. The first rule of the game, *I* always say."

What *was* this? he wondered. A remake of *Bonnie and Clyde?* Her bedroom looked so *frilly.* But then his sidekick, Oscar, had always said he was a sucker for lace curtains and lilac.

"Your point is well taken, Jane. But you really should give some thought to what you're doing, and—"

"No, I shouldn't. That's the second rule. Shoot first, think later. I shouldn't even be talking to you."

"Offhand, I can't think of two people who need to talk more. Why don't you put the gun down?"

"Why don't you go to hell."

At the moment he thought he'd rather be there than in Jane Bailey's bedroom. "Jane, we really do need to talk. Why don't you make some coffee, and—"

"Coffee? You think *I'd* make coffee for *you?*" She shook her head. "Phillip, I don't think you've got a grip on the situation."

"Okay, then I'll make the coffee. Either way, I think you'll find what I have to say very interesting."

"Is that so. So far you've said very little that interests me."

God, she was a hard case. "It's about your brother,"

he coaxed. "It's about Ted, and the reason he was killed."

Those seemed to be the magic words. She stared for a long moment, as though she didn't know what to do. Phillip hoped like hell that she wouldn't make any hasty decisions, and that she, too, wanted some answers. He thought it best to let her go on thinking about it.

Jane looked him straight in the eye. "Who are you, Phillip Decker? Who are you *really?*"

JAYNE CASTLE

excites and delights you with tales of adventure and romance

____TRADING SECRETS

Sabrina had wanted only a casual vacation fling with the rugged Matt. But the extraordinary pull between them made that impossible. So did her growing relationship with his son—and her daring attempt to save the boy's life. 19053-3-15 $3.50

____DOUBLE DEALING

Jayne Castle sweeps you into the corporate world of multimillion dollar real estate schemes and the very private world of executive lovers. Mixing business with pleasure, they made *passion* their bottom line. 12121-3-18 $3.95

If you liked *Romancing the Stone,* you'll <u>love</u>

THE PEREGRINE CONNECTION

Romantic suspense novels for women who enjoy action, danger, mystery, and intrigue mixed up in their romances.

_____ #1 TALONS OF THE FALCON 18498-3-36
_____ #2 FLIGHT OF THE RAVEN 12560-X-24
_____ #3 IN SEARCH OF THE DOVE 11038-6-12

by Rebecca York   **$2.95 each**